AF504373

———————

Mondrala Press wishes to thank all its friends, fans, patrons, and investors for making this book possible, and especially:

Ms. Randa Dumanian
Mr. and Mrs. Karol and Dagmara Maziukiewicz
*de domo* Sowul

without whose enthusiasm and open hearts this book could never have happened.

———————

# THE WHITE JAGUAR

## A TALE OF THE SPANISH MAIN

VOLUME 2
EXODUS

BY ARKADY FIEDLER
TRANSLATED BY TOM PINCH

MONDRALA PRESS

Mondrala Press is an imprint of
Ringel & Esch, S.A.R.L.-S
www.mondrala.com



ISBN epub and kindle:     978-2-919820-54-2
ISBN Paperback:           978-2-919820-55-9
ISBN Hardcover:           978-2-919820-56-6

Edited by Mondrala Press
Cover Design by Mondrala Press

The cover uses elements of a painting by Henri Rousseau, *The Flamingoes*, 1907,
private collection, drawn on the basis of a public domain file served by the
Wikipedia.

The illustrations are taken from J. G. Stedman, *Voyage a Surinam et dans
l'interieur de la Guiane*, Amsterdam, 1798, in the collection of the Tropical
Museum, Amsterdam, obtained thanks to *The Memory Database*, a database
containing paintings, drawings, photographs, sculptures, ceramics, stamps, posters
and newspaper clippings from more than a hundred Dutch museums, archives and
libraries (https://geheugen.delpher.nl).

# ABOUT THE AUTHOR

Arkady Fiedler (1894—1985) was a Polish writer, journalist and adventurer. He studied philosophy and natural science in Kraków, Poznań, and Leipzig. He took part in the Greater Poland Uprising in 1918 and was one of the founders of the Polish Military Organization. He travelled extensively and wrote 32 books which have been translated into 23 languages and sold over 10 million copies in total. His most famous book, *Squadron 303*, about the legendary Polish fighter squadron in the Battle of Britain, sold over 1.5 million copies and was recently published in English by Aquila Polonica Publishing.

# ABOUT THIS BOOK

This is the second episode in a 5 volume series entitled *The White Jaguar*, a fictionalized account of the life and adventures of John Bober, a Virginian renegade and an Arawak chief in Guyana in the first half of the 18th century.

# ABOUT MONDRALA PRESS

Mondrala Press publishes English translations of
great Polish books—books with a track record of international
critical and commercial success but which, for political reasons, have
never been published in English. And now, finally, they are.
Be the first to discover this new territory!

To see our newest titles or to subscribe to our newsletter,
please visit

WWW.MONDRALA.COM
THE GREATEST BOOKS YOU HAVE NEVER HEARD OF

# TRANSLATOR'S SPECIAL REQUEST

Translating and publishing this book has been a labor of love for me.
I grew up reading it, and I have always wanted to be able
to share it with my American friends. And so here it is.
It will not make me rich, but if you liked the book, would you please
recommend it to a friend?
And give it an Amazon review?
https://www.amazon.com/dp/2919820494

THANK YOU!

# THE WHITE JAGUAR

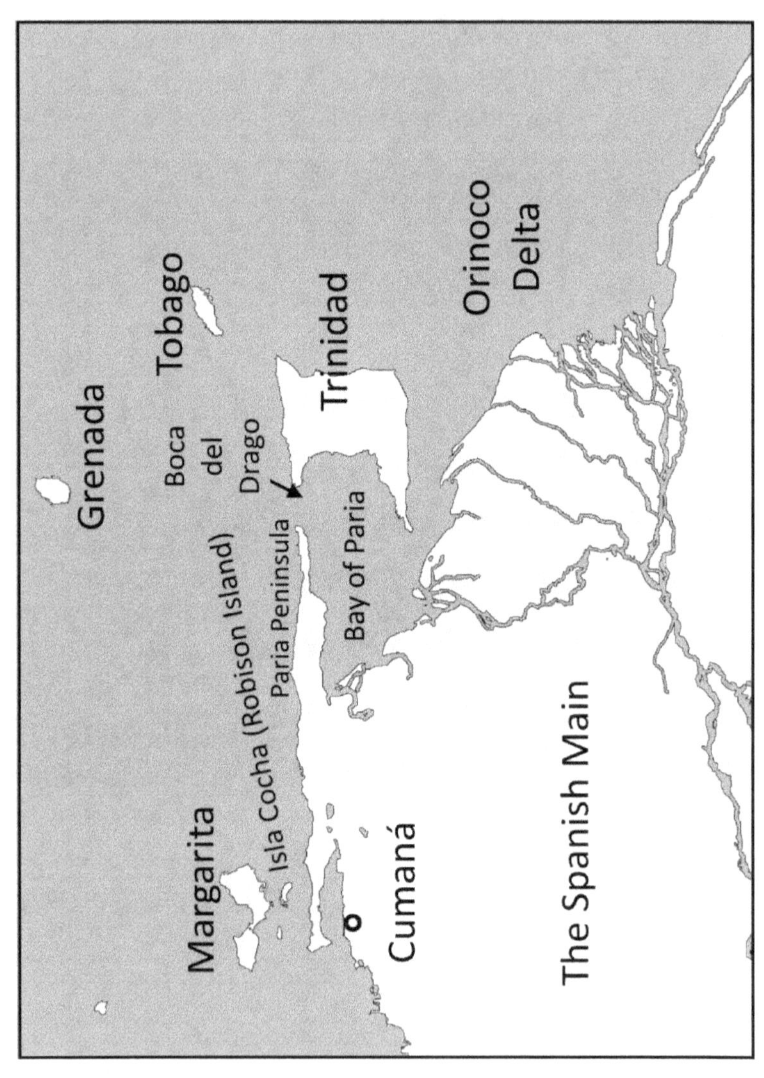


Margarita to Orinoco, 1727

# TABLE OF CONTENTS

# Mateo's Anger

Dodging and covering our tracks, we returned to our cave. The sun was halfway between noon and evening: we did not expect the arrivals to follow us that day.

We had a hearty meal, and then I set about sharpening my hunting knife. This activity and the zeal with which I performed it seemed so bizarre to the boys that at first they stared in disbelief, then looked inquiringly at me, and finally Vagura could not resist asking me in a mocking voice:

"Against whom are you sharpening this dangerous knife?"

"Myself," I said.

He fell silent. After a moment, drawing a finger across his throat, he asked:

"Here?"

"Yes, wise guy!"

He hesitated for a moment, looking for the correct English phrase.

"You want to deprive yourself of your life?"

"No. Just of my beard."

"Ah!" my Indian friends burst out laughing. I've never seen them in such a good mood. Even the usually gloomy Arnak was in good cheer. Both boys knew that in a few hours, regardless of what the big African did, they would meet their countryman Manauri—and that thought filled them with joy.

After sharpening my knife, I located two bamboo slats, and the three of us went down to the river. I smeared my beard with hare fat to soften it, then pinched it between the slats—I had to cut close to the skin.

"You will be less handsome!" Vagura warned me with a troubled expression. "You will look less like a jaguar!"

"Yeah, they will like you less," assessed Arnak.

"Who?"

"Their women. You saw them, no?"

The hooligans laughed at me and my suffering. The knife, though sharp, was no razor: it pulled more hair than it cut. After the beard was gone, it was time for my hair. At the end of the operation, there was still something left on top, but my neck peeked out into the sunlight. When I looked at my reflection in the water after the surgery, I decided I looked more human.

Of course, we hadn't returned to our headquarters for an afternoon snack and a haircut alone. The idea was to hide all the more important items in the event of a burglary. So we dragged both rafts to a safe place, where thick bushes hung like a canopy over the river. We buried our spare guns in the corner of the cave under a pile of stones. We hid what we could in the surrounding bushes, even the several large live turtles that we kept on our farm.

Reassured that our belongings were sufficiently secured, we set off again for the visitors' camp. The sun was just setting when we got there. As long as it was light, we scoured the thicket to avoid ambush. But everything was fine, no one lurked in the bush, the newcomers were encamped in their old place on the other side of the stream.

This time, I stayed behind with two fowling pieces in hand and sent my companions into the camp. They took guns with them so that the others might see that they were armed, but both guns were poor pieces, and they were not loaded: if the boys were to be attacked and have their guns taken away, our visitors would not be able to fire them.

As we parted ways, I gave my young friends my last instructions, like a father saying goodbye to his sons going off on a dangerous mission:

"Talk to Manauri. Do not under any circumstances tell anyone how many of us are here. Not even Manauri should know that. Not yet."

"And what if they will ask?"

"You will answer that I have strictly forbidden you to speak about it. Also, do not reveal how many weapons we have. Assure both Manauri and this African giant that I am not only an honest man but also friendly to both Indians and Africans and will gladly help them if they need me."

"Yes, we will say that," said Arnak. "And it will be the honest truth!"

"Well, all right, then. They are obviously in trouble; something bad has happened to them. It would be the height of folly for them to wage an unprovoked war against us."

"But what if that black giant wants to kill us?"

"I think that is unlikely, if only because of Manauri. But perhaps the African is a madman with no brains? If he threatens you, tell him I've got my gun on him, and he'll get a bullet in his head before he even touches you. All you need to do is shout for help."

"Oh, be very watchful, Yan! We'll try to stand close to the fire so you can keep an eye on us."

"Excellent! And whatever happens, know that I will defend you with my life. I have told you this once before, and now I'll say it again: I will never abandon you in need."

"Yes, you have said it before. We will remember your words."

They left. Darkness was falling fast. I crept after them to the edge of the stream. Here, I clung to the bush. The encampment was several dozen paces away, and I could not just hear every louder word but also see everything clearly, despite the growing dark, because two small fires had been lit in the encampment.

Soon, I heard louder voices. It was the boys arriving at the camp. I saw them walking towards the fire and a crowd of people gathering around them.

And now it was hard for me to see what was happening because so many gathered around them: the huddled figures hid my friends from sight. I looked about me: a coconut tree stood a few paces away. Bent down by the constant onshore wind, the trunk rose diagonally to the height of a man, and only higher did it turn vertical. I climbed the incline, and now, sitting astride it, I had a clear view of the whole camp. The boys were standing by the fire, as they had promised they would. They were about eighty paces away—a bit too much for a sure shot at night. I had one shotgun with me, ready to fire at once. I had left the other one on the ground, leaning it against the trunk of the tree.

I watched Manauri as he met my friends, recognized them, and greeted them with a great show of emotion. He hugged them heartily, as did several other Indians after him, undoubtedly their fellow tribesmen. The Africans also showed joy at the reunion, and even the towering giant, a good head taller than the rest, accepted the young visitors with kindness. At seeing this, a great worry was lifted from my heart, and I awaited further developments with good cheer. Arnak invited his hosts to listen to his tale, and they settled down on the ground to hear him. Only four remained standing: Arnak, Vagura, Manauri, and the African giant.

"Smart cookie," I thought with admiration about my Indian friend because I was sure he had arranged things in this manner so that I would have a better view.

The conversation which followed lasted well into the night, was animated and lively, and quite complicated. First, Arnak went on at length, recounting his experiences on the privateer and on the island. He showed his body full of scars, and Vagura showed the scars on his back and his missing ear. Arnak, of course, spoke Arawak, and Manauri translated into Spanish for the Africans to understand. Then Manauri, in a concise but distinct manner, expounded to my companions his history, connected, as I sensed, with the vast island to the north, for he often pointed in that direction. He spoke with great eloquence. He was evidently an experienced speaker used to addressing large crowds, and his booming voice resounded among the palms and cactus bushes like a brisk mountain stream.

When he finished, Arnak spoke again, and he must have been talking about me now: the Indians listened attentively to his words, but when Manauri translated, there was an unfavorable murmur among the Africans. The giant stepped forward and cursed loudly. The Indians interrupted him and tried to reason. A fierce altercation came of it until Manauri, with a thunderous interjection and a judicious argument, appealed to the quarreling sides to reason and calmed the storm. There was some kind of agreement, a noticeable relaxation, and Arnak came towards me, calling me by name.

I shouted back to him. As he approached, he briefly explained the situation:

"It's all OK, Yan!"

"What was it?" I wondered. "What about that argument?"

"The Arawaks trust you because we have guaranteed for you. And the Africans would be OK with you except..."

"Except?"

"They fear all whites. But we convinced them."

"You think so?"

"Yes, I think so. Yes."

"And why did they come here? What does Manauri say?"

"They came from that island to the north. It is indeed Margarita. We were not mistaken. The Africans and Indians were slaves there, but recently, there was a rebellion. The slaves rebelled, there was a fight, and the slaves lost. Their owners have been hunting them mercilessly. Many have been killed. But these people managed to hijack three boats and rowed away at night. It took them two days to get here."

"And what are they planning to do?"

"Escape to the mainland. Now they just want to rest a little and get some food. They have little left to eat."

"So they will stay here several days?"

"Yes."

"Aren't they afraid of pursuit?"

"Their opinions are divided. They left Margarita at night, and probably no one saw them. So far, they haven't noticed any pursuit. They hope to rest, resupply, and then go on the mainland."

"Do they know about the current?"

"We haven't mentioned it."

Not wanting to look ridiculous lugging about two guns, I took only one with me, slung it over my shoulder, and left the other one leaning against the coconut trunk. I was pretty sure that no one saw it: it was already completely dark. I waded through the ankle-deep water and walked straight to the fire where the elders stood.

"*Buena noche*! Good evening!" Manauri greeted me.

"*Buena noche*!" I replied and, approaching, offered him my hand. He shook it firmly. He was a man of about forty, with a calm, reasonable expression, inspiring easy trust. I replied to his sincere gaze with my best smile.

About a dozen men stood about the fire, Indians and Africans. I approached each one in turn and greeted him with a handshake. The black giant stood aside and was clearly thinking of withdrawing, but I hastened to him and, stretching out my hand, exclaimed:

"*Buena noche, amigo*!"

And since everyone was looking at us, it did not seem proper to refuse to shake my hand. Yet, he barely touched it. His eyes remained fixed on the ground. He was all puffed up like a rooster. An extraordinary intelligence and a kind of defiant pride beamed from his face—and a great stubbornness. But even through this aura of hostile refusal, I could see his good looks and native charm. I was surprised to find that the giant was relatively young: he was not older than twenty-five, a little younger than me.

"*Amigos*!" I addressed myself to all present and switched immediately to English. "Friends! As a castaway on this island for more than a year, I welcome you cordially to my home. I assure you that I will give you all the help I can so that you can regain your freedom."

The speech was quite a hassle because, first, Arnak translated my English into Arawak, then Manauri his Arawak into Spanish. Still, the path, though long and winding, took us home.

The Indians, hearing my words, did not hide their approval. Manauri expressed his thanks and declared that we would all strive for our freedom together because, as Arnak had told him, I also intended to go to the mainland, and since I was a man experienced in the wild and familiar with the island, they would gladly accept my help and listen to my advice.

But here, the African giant sprang forward. He trembled all over, sparks of anger flashing from his eyes.

"People!" he shouted. "Have you lost your mind?! Can't you see he's white? Has any white man ever been your friend?"

"Mateo, calm down," Manauri tried to calm him in a gentle voice.

"Is your memory so short? Do you have the brain of a bird?" the black man objected. "Have you forgotten all the wrong these white monsters have done us? Who branded our cheeks? Condemned us to slavery for life? Who whipped us and tore flesh from our bones? And you want to trust him? You want to take his advice?"

"Just while we are here, on this island," replied someone from among the Indians.

"He is different!" avowed Manauri.

"Why different? How different? He is alone and weak, so he is pretending friendship. But how will he act once we meet other whites? How do you know he's different from the others?"

"Arnak has told us."

"Arnak! Arnak! Or maybe Arnak is a lying dog that eats from his master's hand and will betray his brothers just to please his boss? Have we not seen such traitors? Were not our overseers black? How do you know that Arnak is not one of those traitorous dogs?"

"We have known Arnak since he was a boy!"

"Years ago! Years! Enslavement changes everything!"

"Enslavement has only made him a better man. I can see that!"

"'He's different! He's different!'" mocked Mateo. "Why would he be different? Wasn't he on a pirate ship? He was, Arnak has told us. And don't pirate ships raid peaceful villages and capture people into slavery?" And then he challenged me: "Why were you on a pirate ship? Tell us! You!"

His glowing eyes fixed on me, and he awaited my answer like an implacable judge. When his question reached me, from Spanish to Arawak to English, I replied simply:

"I had to."

"You had to? Were you—a slave?" Mateo jeered.

"Almost a slave. I was running from my master's killers as you are running now from your masters' men. I had no choice but to flee on a pirate ship?"

"How's this? Are there white slaves in your country? It's the first I hear of it."

"He's an Englishman, not a Spaniard! Do not forget about this!" Manauri interjected pleadingly. "The Spaniards don't have white slaves, but the English do. Is it not true?" he turned to me.

Since the question was addressed to me, I explained that it was indeed true. For though we had no white slaves in Virginia, we did white bondsmen, men and women condemned to obligatory service by the court of law or indentured in payment for their Atlantic passage.

"And they work on plantations like other slaves?" snorted Mateo incredulously.

"Yes. They do. Not for life, but for some years until they redeem themselves."

"This is very strange news to me! For my part, I know that the English are no better than the Spanish. On the island of Jamaica, they killed all the Indians and imported thousands of African slaves. They torture them there just like the Spaniards do here. But I haven't heard of white slaves on Jamaica. And you were such a slave? Tell me. Where?"

His derisive, boastful manner started to get on my nerves. I felt a strong urge to spite him. I could have answered that I had been a slave and thus closed the whole matter. But I was conceited. I did not want to humiliate myself by resorting to lies.

"No, I was not such a slave."

"Do you hear? He admits it!" Mateo shouted triumphantly, turning to the Indians.

"But I was hunted," I added in an excited, angry voice. "And I had to flee to save my life! And the only means of escape was to join the pirate ship."

"And you want us to believe you?" Mateo laughed maliciously.

"I do, yes!" I shouted. "I want you to believe me because I am an honorable man, and I take you all for honorable people."

Mateo's face changed, he became serious. He weighed something in his mind for a good moment, staring at the fire. Then he raised his eyes filled with deep concern and said to the Indians:

"Until now, there was an agreement between us. Our common struggle united us. Together, we broke free from captivity and came to this island. Now, a great danger has come our way: this white man has come. The white man has always been our enemy. You say this white man is an exception, a friend..."

"Mateo!" Manauri interrupted him in an imploring voice. "He really is our friend, trust me!"

"How can I trust you when you don't know the man at all? Stop it, stop it, my friend!"

"You have to believe! Try!"

"I can't believe it because there is a thing at stake here that is too important to risk: the fate of all of us. But wait! There is another problem! Let's assume that you're right, Manauri, and that this white man is a decent man. But he's English, right? And all these islands around us, and this mainland where we are going, and this sea—they all belong not to the English but to the Spanish, the enemies of the English. If an Englishman falls here in the Spanish hands, they will deal with him as they will deal with us, and who knows, maybe worse!"

"And therefore, Mateo?"

"A simple thing. He might mean well, for now. But if we go against the Spanish, which may happen soon, and if we have to fight, won't he, the Englishman, suddenly remember that he is a white man first and English only second? Will he not betray us to the Spanish in the moment of our greatest need just to save his own skin? Will he not sell our lives to save his own?"

There was a deafening silence. Mateo's words made a deep impression. They had an incredible, captivating power. He was not only robust in body but also in brains. His train of thought was precise and intelligent, and it was undeniable that any weak and vacillating man in my position might indeed do that—betray the runaway slaves to save himself. Mateo's logic was perfect in every way except one: he misjudged my character.

Arnak now came to my defense. He reminded our guests that we three had come in contact with the Spanish twice before—once when a ship appeared off the coast and could easily have been summoned by smoke and fire; and once when the shipwrecked Spanish, fleeing from their burning ship, landed on the island; and that in those situations I had always acted as a sincere friend of the Indians and an enemy of the Spaniards.

"To suspect this man of inconsistency and low character," concluded Arnak, "is ridiculous and unfair!"

"The situations which you describe," replied Mateo, "are no argument: the white man could have done this or that *then*. He was not cornered or at risk of life. But when he has a knife at his throat, when he can buy his own life by selling us—"

He didn't finish his sentence and left it to his audience to complete it in their heads.

# Secession

Mateo's ferocity and suspicion chilled the souls of the fugitives. His words were ominous and all the more depressing because they were so reasonable.

After a long, awkward silence, Manauri spoke to Mateo:

"So what do you advise us to do? Do you have some suggestion?"

"I do!"

Everyone stared at the black giant intently. He gave me an evil, cold look. I saw the calm, cold stare I had seen in predatory beasts when they readied to pounce on their prey. Involuntarily, I touched my rifle to see if it was still at my shoulder.

"Whether he is a friend or not a friend," growled Mateo, "a good man or a bad man, it doesn't matter now. His very existence is a threat to us. We will only be safe when he is dead!"

When Arnak and Vagura heard these words translated to them, they gave a fierce shout of indignation and grabbed their rifles. In the silence that suddenly fell, there was a loud crack of two drawn cocks.

"Don't be so hasty, boys, don't be so hasty!" Mateo spoke to them sharply. "I have not finished speaking. I know you have some special consideration for this white man. I know that he has bewitched you two and also strangely possessed many adults in our group. So, I will not try to kill him. Long may he live! But I demand something else. To make sure that he can't harm us, let us keep him tied up as long as we're on this island. We'll only release him when we leave. And when we do, we will leave him here."

"No!" Arnak vehemently objected. "That won't happen! You won't tie him up! And we will not leave him here! He will go with us to the mainland."

"Hush, boy!" the giant rebuked him. "Nobody is asking you."

Vagura spoke up in defense of his friend.

"No!" he said passionately, incensed. "We won't let you! We have guns! We have many guns!"

Mateo shrugged, then snorted dismissively:

"That's excellent! I'm glad to hear it. He will need his guns when we leave him here alone!"

Silence fell again. The giant cast an impatient glance at the Indian elders and spoke to them reproachfully:

"These young people have no respect. They strut about, wave their guns, and talk nonsense. And you say nothing."

"You're putting us in a difficult situation," said embittered Manauri.

"I'm putting you in a difficult situation? This white man is putting us in a difficult situation!"

"You're not being reasonable, Mateo."

"Maybe so! But you have to make up your mind. I made my opinion clear. Now, you tell us what you think."

"Very well. Wait then. We will consult!"

And the Arawaks held council together. Everyone spoke. Everyone had an opinion. They spoke in Arawak, so I did not understand much, but I understood that some were firmly behind me while others hesitated.

Whatever they might decide, my position was highly compromising. We were standing near the fire, but the flames, which had not been stoked properly for some time, had died down. Clutching the butt of my shotgun, I glanced vaguely about to see how I could leap into safety if things turned sour. The best remedy, it seemed to me, was to run back across the stream because few people stood in that direction, and if I ran fast, I could disappear in the dark in a few bounds.

Fortunately, I did not have to run. The Indians declared in my favor. Mateo, biting his lip and controlling his agitation with difficulty, heard Manauri's decision. Then he shouted at the top of his voice:

"Do you know what this means? It means..."

"It means," interrupted the Indian, "that we have an ally who can help us get away from here. He can help us with his experience, with his knowledge of the island, and with his weapons, of which he has plenty."

"No, Manauri! I will not agree to it! I don't trust this white man. I will not go with him. Neither me nor my people."

"So what are you going to do? We are not going to fight over this, are we?"

"If you don't change your mind, I and my people will leave. I don't want to hear any more about this white man."

"You will leave us?"

"Yeah, I'm leaving now!"

"You can't be serious, Mateo. Don't joke."

But Mateo was not joking. He had made up his mind, insisted, and there was no arguing with him. The night was coming to an end. Mateo proposed to leave at dawn.

I took Manauri aside and suggested to him to move his party into the vicinity of my cave, where it was easy to get food because of the quick access to Lake Abundance.

"And Mateo, where is he going to go?" I asked.

"I don't know. He alone knows."

"Perhaps he should go to the east side of the island. That way, since my cave is in the west, we will not get in each other's way, and it will be easier for everyone to find enough food."

"Is there any food in the west?"

"Yes. The vegetation is about the same as here, and there are probably more animals because we almost never hunted there. And on the southwestern tip of the island, sea turtles come ashore, and they should feed Mateo's people for many days."

"I'll see what Mateo says to that. I'll talk to him."

Mateo accepted my suggestion because he wanted to be as far away from me as possible. There were very few belongings to divide, mainly the three boats, one larger and two slightly smaller, but there was an ugly ruckus about them. Manauri's party was much larger, with twenty-two people, while Mateo had only fifteen. Nevertheless, he demanded two boats for himself and justified this by the fact that he had more women and children than Manauri did.

"What's the difference?" reasoned the Indian. "You have three women, we have two. You have four children, we have three. And women and children occupy less space in boats than men do!"

"I don't care. We need two boats."

Furious that the Indian had not yielded to him in the matter of the white man, Mateo stuck to his demand in blind anger and was deaf to all arguments. His stubbornness was insurmountable. Wishing to assuage the quarrel and put an end to the strife, I whispered to Manarui to relent.

"We have two rafts. We'll manage somehow," I said. We will have enough rowers to break through the current."

So Manauri agreed to give up the two smaller boats on the condition that he got to keep the largest one, to which Mateo agreed. The giant was clearly gratified to have prevailed.

A pale glow in the eastern sky heralded the end of the night. I sent Vagura across the stream to fetch me the fowling piece which I had left under the palm tree.

The people in the camp got busy gathering their meager possessions while Manauri, Mateo, Arnak, and I remained talking by the fire. Mateo wanted to leave immediately, but I asked him for a moment of his time. I knew the nature of the island and the possibilities of obtaining food here, so the matter of food for so many people—forty-one in all—occupied my mind.

"There isn't enough game here to feed everybody," I said. "It is necessary to collect fruit, wild vegetables, and roots."

"We will do that," said Manauri. "We know the forest."

"Easy for you to say, for you are locals. But Mateo's companions may not know this forest. They come from Africa and have probably spent all their time in this part of the world on a plantation."

"That's not a problem!" exclaimed Manauri. "I'll send two of my people with them, and they will teach them what fruit and vegetables to pick. Besides, Mateo's wife knows about these things: she is one of us."

"I don't want your help!" the giant sneered. "We'll manage fine by ourselves."

At that moment, Vagura came running, all flustered, and whispered in my ear that he had not been able to find my fowling-piece. It had disappeared.

"I left it leaning against the trunk of the palm tree," I explained. "How could you have missed it?"

"I looked everywhere—under your palm tree, then, just to make sure, under several others. The gun is gone!"

"You didn't look properly!"

"Come and see for yourself!"

I went. And indeed, my fowling piece was gone. Someone had taken it. Let's call it by name: someone had stolen it. I felt bitter anger. I was resentful.

Returning to the encampment, I told Manauri about my loss. The Indian immediately inquired among his people.

"Nobody has seen it," he reported.

I went to Mateo and told him to his face that my fowling piece had been stolen.

"I know," he leered at me. "I have it. My men brought it to me. I will keep it."

"It is my gun, you realize."

"I know."

"Oh?" I made big eyes at him, irritated.

Mateo returned to the Indians as if taking them for witnesses.

"Now you see for yourselves what kind of a friend this white man is. He says he has many guns. He knows what kind of trouble we're in and that we need weapons. But he is asking for his gun back."

And then he turned to me:

"No. It's my gun now!"

With supreme effort, I managed to control my anger. I took a deep breath, and I looked regretfully at Mateo.

"Mateo!" I said in a low voice, looking him directly in the eyes. "You're on a dangerous path! I know that you need weapons. But it is one thing to ask, and another thing is to steal. Had you asked me for that gun, man to man, I certainly wouldn't have refused you."

Seeing his angry expression, I added:

"At any rate, that gun is not much use to you. It has one single charge. You fire it once, and then it's all over."

"Perhaps you want me to go down on my knees and beg you for shot and powder?" he growled angrily in reply.

"I'm not asking that, Mateo! And because I see that you'll need a gun, I will give you powder and bullets from my stores."

A murmur of appreciation rippled among the Indians and Africans. But for Mateo, my words were like a goad. His eyes sparkled in a fit of passion, and he shook his fists.

"Look at him, the benefactor!" he shouted. "Don't you humiliate me with your generosity! Don't you make a fool of me! I don't want your gunpowder! In fact, I don't want your stupid gun, either! I hope you choke on it!"

He called to his men to bring him the gun, and he ordered them to hand it over to me. His people were slow to do so, and Manauri entreated him to be reasonable and take the gun, but Mateo was not to be assuaged.

It was getting brighter. The horizon glowed with the first rays of sunlight. I climbed a nearby dune and studied the ocean. It was empty as far as the eye could see. There was no pursuit in sight.

Eleven of the Indian party—the women and children and six rowers—boarded the Indian boat, and the rest of us set out on foot. Mateo intended to row around the northern tip of the island. I advised him not to do so: the opposite direction—south then west—was a little quicker and, above all, safer, for if any pursuit were to come, it would come from the north, from Margarita. The giant just shook his head and muttered that he would go north anyway.

As they boarded their boats, someone pointed out Mateo's

wife to me. She was a young and very beautiful Indian woman. She held in her arms a baby boy who was perhaps about a year old. Mateo took the baby from her with extraordinary care, which I would never have expected from such a surly man, and carefully helped her into the boat. When his eyes rested on his wife and child, his face became imbued with such a profound expression of love and devotion that I couldn't get enough of the view.

Manauri approached me and asked me if we should cover the traces of the encampment.

"Absolutely," I replied.

We buried the remains of the fire and used palm fronds to sweep the sand to erase our footprints.

Later, as we walked south along the shore and I looked out to sea, I saw that all boats headed south—both the Indian boat and the two African boats. So Mateo had followed my advice after all.

"What a strange man!" I thought to myself.

# The Long Shadow of Margarita

Despite the sleepless night, there was no time to rest. We were under a lot of stress: twenty-five mouths to feed in our circumstances was not a trifle.

As soon as we dragged the big boat up the brook (which we did at high tide, and everyone had to help) and hidden it under vegetation, I ran to the cornfield, which had stood unattended for twenty-four hours. I took Manauri with me: I wanted to impress him with our agricultural achievement.

My worst fears proved correct: a swarm of parrots sat on the ripening cobs, and the rascals gorged themselves with gusto. A large flock of black groundbirds frolicked down below, pecking at the lower cobs like hens. I wanted to chase them away, but Manauri stopped me.

"We'll have a bird hunt!" he whispered to me in Spanish, which I could easily understand from his expressive gestures.

"Right!" I said more to myself than to him.

Without leaving the thicket, we turned back and ran to the cave. Everyone snatched whatever fell to hand: some took bows and arrows, others javelins or maces or sticks. The hunters set up waiting in a line at the edge of the forest, and the beaters rushed into the field from the side of the river. We were extraordinarily lucky. The parrots, of course, screeched and flew away, and only a few were shot with arrows. But we caught the black groundbirds easily and clubbed them to death. This took place amid such merry shouting and laughter that you would think it was a carnival at a fairground. We took our successful hunt as a good omen for our future.

The women at once began cooking the birds and soon served us a tasty breakfast. But we didn't waste time feasting and set about dividing work immediately. Consulting with Manauri at every step, we soon established that we would send out two parties of hunters, one guided by Arnak and the other by Vagura.

One group would go inland, to Lake Abundance, and the other north, to the Parrot Grove. Two fishermen, armed with spears, would go out on a raft to fish near the rocks where the Spanish brigantine had burned. The oldest Indian, a man of about fifty, would remain in the camp and, with the help of the women, build huts for us to sleep in, and our best archer would guard the cornfield. An Indian who had served on Margarita as a carpenter would try to enlarge our second raft and hew new oars with the axe. And I?

The issue of security and defense gnawed at me. Even if there was no pursuit from Margarita, we would be exposed to other dangers once we reached the mainland—and that required planning. We had eight unused guns. This priceless resource had to be harnessed. Eight guns in good hands, together with our three, made eleven: a devastating volley in any small engagement. It was only necessary to make it usable: to train people. I turned to Arnak:

"Arnak, ask our people if any are familiar with firearms!"

"Europe Bestowing its Blessings on Africa and America"

Not everyone understood my question.

"Has anyone here shot a gun before?"

Three raised their hands.

"Can you look after a gun? Clean, load, aim, fire?"

They nodded.

"I need five volunteers to learn how to shoot. Anyone?"

Everyone applied. All were eager to learn the art. Owning a gun was every Indian's dream. Manauri chose four men. He himself was the fifth.

Since I wanted to set to work immediately, it was necessary to change the assignment of tasks, especially of the hunting parties. Then, after everyone had gone to their assignment, I set to work near the cave with my eight students.

I admired the zeal of these Indians. Long familiar with the opinion of the Virginian colonists concerning the alleged indolence of the natives and having heard over and over from my fellow sailors how lazy and stupid the natives of South America were, I could not help but be amazed at the wit and diligence of my new companions. A different world was opening before me, a new understanding of man.

It did not seem likely to me that the intelligence and enthusiasm of my companions had been somehow imparted to them by the Spanish during their captivity. As I thought about it more, it seemed to me that slavery could only have crushed the human spirit rather than upraised it. No, it was something else: it was their desire for freedom—the one great, invincible force of the human heart! These people wanted to be free. That was why they undertook their dangerous flight, worked, learned, and why their eyes sparkled with enthusiasm. They saw their road to freedom wide open before them, they had a vision of a bright tomorrow, and that hope and vision filled them with energy and made them new, stronger people.

As once long ago, when I had lain wounded by the jaguar and watched Arnak and Vagura take care of me, so now, too, the sight of my Indian companions made me think of my countrymen in Virginia. And again, a bitter resentment welled up in me, a resentment for their easy, unthinking prejudice. How many of my people hated and deprecated Indians sight unseen, on nothing but hearsay! Oh, if only those blind men were now in my place and saw Manauri and his friends striving to master their guns!

In teaching my students, I put special emphasis on the ability to load quickly, aim, and keep the powder dry and well-protected from rain. Only after I saw them get handy at cleaning and loading did we start shooting. I let each shoot twice, first with a small amount of powder so as not to startle the shooter with a bang, then with a normal charge. They were diligent students, and after a few hours of hard work, they learned a great deal. It would be difficult to call them skilled shooters, but I felt that I could entrust them with our guns as long as they remained under constant supervision.

"We'll practice for at least an hour a day, but without shooting," I said. "We must conserve gunpowder!"

Because there were still some hours left until sunset, Manauri and some men went into the forest to cut branches and vines for bows and reeds for arrows. I was very happy about it because with so many of us, bows would have to remain the main weapon of our group, and it was necessary to have as many of them as possible and of good quality.

Since I remained near our cave all day, I climbed to the top of our hill about every hour or so or sent whoever was to hand up to look for any sign of an approaching ship. But the sea remained sparkling clean and peaceful: there was no sign of any threat anywhere. I constantly made sure that we took all precautions, for I felt obliged to do so, both as the oldest inhabitant of the island and, therefore, a kind of a host; and as the man entrusted by Providence with the safety of these people so severely tested by fate.

Toward evening, our hunters began to arrive. They carried a variety of prey: there were "bunnies" and all kinds of birds and lizards and even snakes. There were a few baskets of fruit and berries—but we had too few baskets and needed to pleat more. I learned that the tips of some palm trees were considered a delicacy: one cut them just above where the hardened, wooden part of the trunk ended. Boiled in water, they tasted delicious.

The fishermen who had gone to the Five Rocks caught a few fish there—but really, just a few, for they had had an exciting adventure with a seal or similar creature and nearly brought us a mountain of meat. They managed to jab the animal with a javelin and almost had it in their power, but at the last moment, it broke free.

During supper, we discussed our plans for the following day. We set up a permanent watch on the hilltop and decided to send a raft with a few hunters to catch turtles on the west side of the island. They would have a chance to see how Mateo and his people fared.

I was curious about the details of life on Margarita. I found out that there were many Spanish plantations there, but most Spaniards lived off pearl fishing. The coast of the sea had a rocky bottom to which strange pearl-producing mussels clung: a species so precious to the few and so cursed by the many. Not every clam contained a pearl: hundreds had to be cut off with a knife and lifted from the depths of the sea to find just one costly pearl.

Only slaves were used as divers. It was such harmful work that even the healthiest of men died of lung disease within a year. A diver who became sick was doomed to death, his life was forfeit, his last months lived in inhuman torment, gasping for air.

As a result of such high mortality, the Spaniards on Margarita were constantly short of slaves, constantly organized manhunts all over the Caribbean, and imported Africans at high prices whenever they could. Amid all this, a kind of madness of cruelty developed in them. They mistreated the slaves at every turn, dealing them the most severe punishments at the slightest opportunity. Meeting out and watching elaborate tortures became a kind of a sport.

When the Indians told me this, I must have looked incredulous. They noticed this and showed me their mutilated bodies, backs scored with flogging rods, hands missing fingers, deep scars on legs, arms, and chests.

It was the first time I came so close to the monstrous world of slavery. There had been slavery back in my country, too, in my Virginia, and some people mistreated and tormented their slaves, but I had never seen it with my own eyes. Living in the western woods, among free settlers, I had never seen slavery or even stopped to think about it at all, and now I felt like I received a sharp rap on the head. When I looked at these people, I could not believe that they had had to serve others like working beasts of burden and that they had been destined to die a merciless death on someone else's orders.

That evening, by the fire on my Robinson Island, for the first time in my life, I saw with painful clarity all the injustice that existed in the world. And who perpetrated it, who brought so many atrocities into the world?

"Would you like to hear," Manauri asked me, "how Mateo's brother died?"

"Tell me."

Mateo's brother had been a diver for the richest Spaniard on the island, a Don Rodrigues, whose very name seemed to give my guests a shudder. His master constantly demanded that he should be more diligent in extracting shells from the sea, but the diver could not work any harder, for he had been working for ten months and was at the end of his strength. His master, seeing that he would not get much use out of him anymore and wanting to set an encouraging example for his other divers, sentenced him to death. Dogs were his choice of weapon. The Spanish had big dogs on Margarita, all specially trained for the purpose. On the day of the sentence, the master invited some Spaniard friends, rounded up all his slaves, even little children, and served them a bloody spectacle. In the arena of his courtyard, he ordered a dangerous dog to be set on the convict. Mateo's brother defended himself against the beast as best he could, even though both he and everyone else knew that his hour had come. He stayed on his feet, keeping the enraged dog from his throat with his bare hands. When his master had had enough of the spectacle, he ordered a second dog to be released. The poor man had to succumb to two dogs. While he was fending off the first, the second caught up with him, knocked him to the ground, and ripped his throat out. They were terrible, hateful, cruel dogs, just like their masters.

"Go to rest now!" I asked the Indians as silence fell. "We have much hard work tomorrow. And remember that here, on my island, you are quite safe. Sleep easy!"

Even though I wished them a good night's sleep, I myself long tossed and turned before I fell asleep. The shocking tale had taken a toll on my nerves.

# The Sign of the Vulture

The following day, everyone was up at dawn, and after a quick meal, we each went to our tasks. I was on my way to the corn patch to see if there had been any pests at night when our Indian scout, who had spent the night on top of the hill, came running breathless and waving his arms:

"The Spanish! The Spanish!"

I did not need to speak Spanish to understand.

I flew back to the camp, already abuzz with the news, and quickly climbed up the hill in the company of the Indian. We did not have to go all the way to the top: barely fifty feet up, we saw them.

"Over there!" my companion pointed.

A ship was coming from the north. It was still ten or twelve miles away, but it headed straight for our coast. It would reach us in two or three hours. It had two masts, which I guessed made it a schooner, a swift ship, much smaller than the brigantines common in these waters.

"Get everyone back here! Someone go fetch the hunters!" I called to the Indian, forgetting that he did not understand English.

There were four adults left in the camp: the Indian who told us about the ship, two women, and me. The hunters had left in four parties, and each had to be warned and brought back: Arnak had led a group inland to Lake Abundance, Vagura north to Parrot Grove, Manauri had taken one raft and sailed south for turtles, and the fishermen went back to Five Rocks on the second raft—the Five Rocks lay offshore about a mile to the north of us. With gestures, facial grimaces, and names, I explained who was to run to whom to turn him back, and I chose the most complicated task for myself: that of finding Arnak in the interior of the island. The hunters had left the camp about a quarter of an hour earlier, so we expected to catch them quickly. Unfortunately, the fishermen had left long before dawn and had been fishing at Five Rocks all morning.

Everyone ran on his mission. Both women were relatively young and healthy, so they did not disappoint. After about an hour, one brought Vagura's party, the other Manauri's, which, paddling near the shore, saw the woman signaling to them from the shore. Just as they finished hiding their raft in the bushes by the stream, I returned with Arnak's party.

"Still no fishermen!" noticed anxiously.

The scout from the hill had gone to fetch them. As he was an excellent swimmer (of which he had assured me with exaggerated gestures), I had ordered him to swim to Five Rocks, some half a mile offshore.

The Spaniards on the ship must have had a spyglass, so I forbade my people to appear anywhere near the seashore or in any open spaces in general—and this was especially true about our scouts on the hill.

We extinguished all fires. I checked our weapons. How glad I was that I had not neglected to teach those few Indians about guns the day before! Now, I gave each his gun, the stronger fellows the heavy muskets, and I ordered them to load. I gave each one a portion of powder and bullets, enough for ten shots. After this ceremony, I declared that each man should guard and protect his gun and his ammunition with his life and that I entrusted the guns to them only for the time being.

"The fishermen aren't back yet?" I asked Manauri.

"No."

Manauri sent two runners to see what had happened to the fishermen and the scout who had gone to fetch them.

There was no doubt that the schooner—the ship was indeed a schooner—was aimed at our island. It was now about a quarter of a mile from the shore and still heading straight toward us. Hiding behind the boulders on the mountainside, we watched it with bated breath.

"It's approaching the Five Rocks!" said Arnak.

"Look!" I whispered back. "They dropped the main sail."

"They're coming ashore?"

"I think so."

But no, the schooner did not drop anchor. It didn't stop—it just slowed down. Apparently, the Spanish wanted to take a closer look at our island. Looking at them through my spyglass, I saw a bunch of men standing by the side of the ship and straining their eyes toward the shore. One of them held a spyglass. Yes, these Spaniards had come in pursuit of the runaway slaves! I tried to count them. I reckoned there were about fifteen.

I tried not to show it, but I trembled in my heart. A dozen Spaniards armed to their teeth, perhaps with a pack of trained attack dogs—they could easily defeat our group, even though we were more numerous. They would defeat us because we were poorly armed, and no one except me had seen much fighting. I did not place as much hope as before in the usefulness of my freshly minted musketeers and wondered whether bows would not be the more suitable weapon in their hands. I confided these concerns to those present on the hill: Manauri, Arnak, and Vagura.

"I think," replied Arnak, "that these three, who have handled guns before, will not fail us."

"But the others?"

"Who knows."

"What do you think, Manauri?

"These three will be alright. The others—you know yourself."

"Shall we give them bows as well as guns?"

"Yes. Everyone in our group can shoot a bow."

"I've got an idea. Let's do this. Six of us will shoot: those three, Arnak, Vagura, and me. The others will clean and load the guns for us so that we can shoot faster."

"Yes, that's a better idea," they all agreed.

Meanwhile, the ship had cleared the Five Rocks and was slowly approaching us. The second sail, not lowered, was more and more clearly outlined against the azure of the ocean. In its whiteness, it resembled a dove, and I shuddered at the ridiculousness of the simile: it was not the sign of a dove but the mark of a rapacious vulture, the personification of impending death, the specter of bloodthirsty oppressors. The ship was moving very slowly. There was so much latent menace in its stealth that even I, watching from afar, was involuntarily holding my breath.

"They will have dogs!" I said. "How many poisoned arrows do we have?"

"About thirty."

"And the poison has not lost its kick?"

"We won't know until we try."

After a moment, Arnak added emphatically:

"They can have dogs, but the men are worse!"

"What?"

"Let's save the poisoned arrows for the men."

"Yes, you're right."

The schooner was just opposite our hill now, a quarter of a mile from the shore and less than half a mile from us. Looking through the spyglass, I could see it as clearly as if in the palm of my hand. I counted the men once again: fifteen. I didn't see any dogs. If there were any, they were not visible. The men were on deck and watching the shore. From their relaxed movements, I sensed that they had not yet seen anything and were not preparing to go ashore. But they watched the shore like hawks. As the ship passed us and moved south, our tension eased slowly.

We went down, leaving only two Indians at the top. They were supposed to report to us every hour.

The poison on the arrows has not yet lost its power: a scratched bunny died after a few moments.

At last, the fishermen returned, along with the Indian sent to fetch them. Their story was quite frightening. They noticed the ship very late when it was at most half a mile from the rocks. They immediately jumped in the water. Lest they be discovered, they swam beside the raft, keeping it between themselves and the ship. They pushed her very slowly so as not to attract attention. Thus, they reached the shore, and there they hid the raft and themselves among some rocks protruding into the sea.

"You are complete morons!" Manauri rebuked the fishermen. "To let your enemy get so close to you unobserved! Do you think they saw you? The raft is an obvious giveaway."

"I don't think they saw us. There is much seaweed and other debris floating between the Five Rocks. We threw some seaweed onto our raft to make it look like a piece of flotsam."

In the face of danger, the Indians took on a militant vigor: a dormant warrior spirit woke up in them. An enthusiasm to fight the hated enemy seized the whole group. The three hunting groups transformed automatically into three military squads: groups of warriors led by Manauri, Arnak, and Vagura. This happened naturally, for all came from the same Arawak tribe and had known each other for years, if not ever. As for Vagura, Manauri had doubts about his ability to lead because of his young age and asked me for my opinion.

"Let him lead! Do not think about his age but about his life experience. He is wise. You can trust his judgment."

The schooner, meanwhile, continued south at the same slow pace as before, but upon reaching the southeast end of the island, it did not turn westward as we had expected but turned away from the shore and, putting up its sails, headed out to sea, first east, then south, towards the mainland.

"They're circling us like a vulture!" I said. "They're making sure you haven't escaped to the mainland."

"Perhaps, when they don't see us there, they will give up and turn back?" Manaur said.

Vain hope! The ship, breaking through the current, reached the mainland but, finding the shore empty, soon turned around and came back to our island. It resumed its search of the south shore from the same spot where it had left off. We realized then that the Spaniards intended to circumnavigate the whole island.

The day was leaning into the evening. It was about two hours till sunset.

The schooner was now moving west in the direction of Mateo's encampment. They had not been warned; they could not have seen the ship until now because it had been on the east side of the island. They probably hadn't taken proper precautions.

Manauri shared my concern.

"We have to warn them," he said.

When I considered the position of the African party, I became quite alarmed. We knew roughly where Mateo camped because Arnak had described Turtle Point to him. There was a spring of fresh water there, which flowed into a small bay, and Mateo's group had probably set up camp there. As the Spaniards cleared the tip of the island and sailed up along the western shore, would they not spot them easily?

"Let's send someone to warn them right away," I said. "There is no time to lose!"

"Yes! But who?"

# Distant Guns

As long as the Spanish schooner stayed on the other side of the island, our camp was safe. It was enough to leave a small crew here. In the west, though, if the Spaniards spotted the fugitives, there would be a fight. A larger force was needed.

At a hastily called war council in which everyone participated, I submitted a plan of action, the best I could see. I suggested that Manauri and his party should stay behind with three guns while Arnak and Vagura and their men would go west with me. By strenuous march, I hoped to reach Mateo by nightfall, before the Spaniards, who would probably drop anchor at dusk.

Manauri objected to my plan. He was a man in his prime, one of the chiefs of his tribe, a brave, ambitious, and energetic man. He did not want to be left behind when matters of such importance were to be decided.

"There will be fighting there," he said, offended. "How could you think that I would remain in the camp with the women and children?"

I realized that I had committed an indiscretion and wounded his warrior pride. I apologized profusely to him and laid out the reasoning upon which I had based my plan:

"There may be a fight there, but not necessarily so! I hope we can warn Mateo in time and hide his boats. But the Spaniards do have a fast ship and could return to this side of the island before us. Our women and children should not be left unprotected."

"But why would the Spaniards return here?"

"Manauri, have you thought carefully about what our fishermen said this morning? The ship reached within half a mile of the Five Rocks before they spotted it and dived. Did the Spaniards see them? We don't know. They didn't immediately give chase, that's true, but so what? Maybe they wanted to see if there were more fugitives elsewhere on the island? And if they don't find anyone on the other side of the island, might they not come back here? But never mind the possibility. You should come with us, Manauri, but someone has to stay here for defense."

Manauri accepted my apology and then asked his people

whether anyone volunteered to stay behind. No one wanted to stay; everyone wanted to fight. So Manauri, by his authority as a tribe elder, appointed four men, two of them with guns. He had a lot of influence with his men. They obeyed him.

I assigned twenty cartridges per shotgun to the shooters. We took two days' provisions and set off without delay. We distributed the guns and the poisoned arrows evenly between the three teams.

With a brisk step, half walking, half running, we set off, moving single file, as Indians do. There were sixteen of us: we made a long chain. We had nine shotguns, and I took the captain's old pistol.

We covered quite a distance by nightfall. We rested for a while near a spring. I took the opportunity to bring up a point which I considered too important not to make clear: the question of who would command us in battle.

"I was thinking the same thing," said Arnak. "It has to be you!"

"No, I said. By seniority, leadership belongs to Manauri. He is our chief."

Manauri remained silent for a moment, looked at me with a benevolent eye, and then a playful flash flickered in his eyes :

"Ho, ho, slyboots! You mean to tickle my vanity?"

"No, I mean it, honestly," I replied. "You are the chief of the tribe, and you can command them in their language."

The Indian chuckled quietly.

"Ah, Yan, you don't have to flatter us! You are our brother."

Then he turned to his men, pointing to me with his thumb:

"We have been on this island for two days, he for more than a year. He knows every nook and cranny here. He was a great hunter in the forests of his homeland. He provided us with firearms. Who will guide us better against the Spaniards? You say! Am I not right to say that he should lead?"

The Indians nodded in agreement. Manauri assumed the appearance of a troubled man forced to submit to the majority.

"Do you hear?" he turned to me. "They have spoken! They

want you to lead. So you don't mind, do you?"

"No," I replied, amused. I realized how Manauri saw the situation: the fight, if there was going to be one, would be a risky affair. And therefore, not only was it best to appoint a leader with military experience, but it was also wise for Manauri to evade responsibility for the uncertain outcome. And he could do that easily by deferring to me as the host on my island.

Before we resumed our march, I thought it necessary to give some general pointers:

"I repeat: I do not think there will be a fight because I do not think the Spaniards will come ashore. But if, for any reason, they should land, our first and most important priority will be to remain hidden for as long as possible. Not to be seen, not to be recognized. You are all warriors, so you know the value of the element of surprise. Therefore, for as long as we can, we will use only knives, clubs, bows, and poisoned arrows—to make as little noise as we can. And only as a last resort will we fire our guns."

The night had fallen. There was no moon, but the sky was cloudless, and we were able to continue moving by the ample starlight. We walked effortlessly along the shore, a path Arnak, Vagura, and I had already traveled several times. Hour after hour passed, we measured the passage of time by the movement of the stars. About midnight, the moon rose in the east, and it became so light that I ordered our men to watch the sea for any sign of the ship.

From the thicket came the sharp whistling of crickets and the screeches of other insects intoxicated by the hot night; from the sea came the muffled roar of the waves; ridiculously beautiful coconut palms bathed in the silver moonlight, swaying overhead in a racket of their gigantic fronds. All this, and our rapid progress in total and complete silence, led us all into a kind of drowsy trance. We had to constantly pull ourselves out of this half-dream in order not to fall asleep while walking.

We had long since passed the bay where I had first met the two boys and were about to reach our destination. There was about a mile or a mile and a half left between us and Turtle Point.

Suddenly, Arnak, who led our procession, stopped so abruptly that I bumped into him.

"Quiet!" he hissed sharply in a whisper. "Quiet! All stop!"

We all froze, listening.

After a while, we heard a suspicious sound in the distance, distorted by muffled echoes. One thunder, then another, then a pause, followed by a rumble again. There was not a shadow of a doubt: it was the distant roar of gunfire. It came from the vicinity of Turtle Point.

"They've landed!" Arnak whispered.

"We're too late!" someone groaned.

A shock came upon us. Mateo and his men! And now an imminent danger hung over us, much sooner than we had expected: we were stunned by the swiftness of the blow.

We heard more shots before us. No command was necessary. We all started running.

# The Hothead Raisuli

The shooting continued, though the shots were fired with decreasing frequency. As we got closer, we heard them better and could now tell that the shots did not come from one place but from several different directions. They were all in front of us, but some farther from us, some nearer, some directly in front, and some a little to the right, as if in the depths of the island.

Our headlong race had no clear aim, and it could easily have ended fatally: it could have thrown us panting and unable to fight straight into the hands of the Spaniards. I ordered my men to stop and catch their breath.

"What is going on over there, in front of us?" asked Vagura. For a while now, there had been no more shots.

"Don't you understand?" Arnak bristled. "They're chasing them all over the forest."

"Spaniards chasing Mateo's people?"

"Who else?"

One of the Indians asked whether it made sense to go on. Maybe Mateo's group had been wiped out?

"So... we just go back to camp and catch some sleep?" I shuddered.

"We'll pick up the others and hide in the center of the island."

"But is Mateo's group lost? Maybe some have escaped and are hiding in the bush? We should come to their aid."

Arnak supported my position:

"What do you want to do? Do you think you can hide from them? On this island? It's too small! They will find us!"

"They won't know that we are here."

"They won't know? They won't force Mateo's men to tell them?"

I did not want to make any decision until I was sure of the opinion and support of my people. So I asked them what they wanted to do.

"To withdraw now would be stupid," replied Manauri. "The only thing to do is to keep going!"

"And your men? Do they think the same?"

"We all do!" someone whispered with emphasis. There was no more resistance. All nodded assent.

Suddenly, we pricked up our ears: we heard other, new sounds. Despite the usual racket of the tropical night, we all caught clearly that peculiar sound. And there was no doubt as to what that was, either.

"Dogs!" a whisper went through our group.

Once again, I reminded my men of the instruction I had given them beforehand:

"Remember: only bows, javelins, clubs, and knives! And guns only on my command. The Spaniards should not suspect that we have them until it is too late."

"But, Yan!" whispered Arnak: "How are we supposed to communicate if we become separated but are not allowed to shout?"

"You're a smart fellow, Arnak! I forgot about signalization! What should we do?"

A certain species of cricket made short, incessantly repeated whistles: *tss, tss, tss*! They were easy to imitate. Our warning signal became three times *tss* for near distances and the call of the black cuckoo—*pyong*!—for longer distances.

We made good progress through the bush now, even though it was spiky and full of agaves and cacti. The bush was not dense, its branches rarely joined together, and it often gave way to barren clearings. Arnak guided us expertly. I watched his leadership with admiration. He delivered in spades in the hour of need.

The bright moon lit our way, but it could also easily betray our presence. We tried to stay in the shade wherever possible.

We heard dogs barking here and there. We were getting closer, and they would soon be able to sniff us out. I was plagued with doubts. I had taken these men on a perilous quest, and by doing so, I exposed them to mortal danger. My conscience nagged me. I was troubled by the meagerness of our weapons compared to what the Spaniards had. We were in way over our heads.

I watched my companions carefully. Arnak, at the head of the line, was clearing our way. There was a grim courage and fierceness in his face, and his every move expressed a great force of will. Manauri had a stubbornness in his pursed lips that I had never seen in this normally calm, laid-back Indian. Vagura listened intently to the sounds of the night and had a poisoned arrow already nocked in his bow. The man behind him, whose name was Raisuli, was one of the three Indians long acquainted with firearms. With a musket and a club slung over his back and a bow in his hand, he walked as if possessed. His glowing eyes scanned the forest for any trace of the enemy.

I sighed with relief: I understood that no force could stop these people. They were going to fight not because of me but because it was

46

their only way to freedom. I was ashamed to have doubted them even for a moment.

A clearing shone before us in the moonlight. Sparse grass grew in clumps here and there, but the rest was bare sand, and, as was the case with many clearings on the island, it was at most a gunshot across, but it stretched in a straight line almost to the sea, a good thousand paces long. We stopped to discuss in whispers whether to cross the open space or go around it when from the brush on the opposite side came the sharp cracking of branches and the barking of a dog.

"It's coming towards us!" whispered Arnak.

"Take cover!" hissed Manauri.

And just at that moment, from the thicket opposite us ran out into the clearing... not a dog, but a man. He stumbled and fell but got up immediately and ran towards us again. It was obvious that he was running with the last of his strength, his knees buckling under him. As he came closer, we realized he was a she: a black girl from Mateo's group.

She was barely halfway through the clearing when a huge black dog came tearing after her from the forest. In a few leaps, it overtook the woman and jumped on her from behind. The woman didn't even scream—she let out a strangled groan as she fell.

And then everything happened like a flash of lightning. An Indian from Vagura's host darted out into the clearing, drawing his bow as he ran. Before the dog could sink its fangs into the woman's neck, the archer released an arrow from a distance of fifteen paces. The beast, pierced through, wheezed furiously, bit the arrow, and fell limp in a few instants. The Indian grabbed the dazed woman and, holding her under his arm, returned to us in several mighty leaps.

A happy murmur of admiration rewarded the daredevil's feat. The huge dog was still moving, but we could see it was dying and trembling in its last convulsions. The four-legged terror of slaves was dying! Suddenly, Raisuli, standing right behind me, went berserk. He began to dance and shout something at the top of his voice. His companions jumped on him and covered his mouth with their hands, pinned him to the ground, and silenced him.

"What was that?" I asked Arnak.

"Nothing. He was just happy to see the dog die."

Suddenly our attention was focused on the bush on the other side of the clearing. Again, a figure was breaking through the thicket. It must have been the dog's handler: he whistled every now and then. As he reached the edge of the clearing, he stopped.

The dog was still alive and moving its head. The man spotted the animal and dashed to the center of the clearing.

"A Spaniard!" someone in our group whispered.

"Quiet!" hissed Manauri.

The Spaniard, coming close and seeing the dog lying limply, let out a muffled exclamation of surprise. He bent over the animal and turned its body over. It must have been then that he discovered the arrow, for he sprang to his feet and, for a moment, fixed his keen eyes on us.

At that very moment, several arrows whirred softly in the air. They must have all struck home because the distance was no more than thirty paces. The Spaniard fell without uttering a sound. He must have been hit in the throat because as he fell, we heard hoarse wheezing. Before we could stop the hothead, Raisuli ran out into the clearing, brandishing his club, ran up to the man, and smashed his head in with a terrible blow. He didn't have to do that: the fallen man was probably already dead. But that was not all. The Indian must have lost his senses in this moment of triumph. Instead of returning to us quickly, he stayed with the fallen. He began to dance some insane victory dance. He had completely lost all sense of reality.

We stood in a dumb stupor and watched the amazing phenomenon helplessly. Arnak laid down his weapon and prepared to spring out into the clearing. But—he didn't make it. A shot rang out from the other side of the thicket. Raisuli staggered in his mad dance, flipped, and fell motionless to the ground, killed on the spot.

# Two More Spaniards

Two Spaniards stepped into the clearing. They held long guns in their hands; one of them, it seemed to me, was still smoking from its barrel. They did not suspect our presence at all. All their attention was absorbed by the darkening corpses in the middle of the clearing. They were going straight towards them. So far, they had not realized the danger they were in. They seemed to be arguing loudly over something.

"Ask Manauri what they are saying," I said to Arnak.

We stood so close we could easily communicate in whispers. After a while, Arnak breathed into my ear:

"Manauri says one is berating the other because the shot was all wrong."

"It wasn't wrong. Raisuli is dead."

"Yes, but the man was supposed to shoot his legs, not kill him."

"Ah, they wanted the slave alive!"

"Yes!"

"So maybe the other Africans are still alive!"

It gave us some hope that the shots we'd heard so far hadn't necessarily meant the deaths of Mateo's men. But there was no time to reflect.

As the two Spaniards approached the corpse, we saw them freeze suddenly. Only now did they recognize their fallen comrade. They tried to lift him and saw that the Spaniard was dead.

We had to act quickly, before they came to their senses.

"Arnak! Shoot!"

"I know!" the youth whispered back.

Quick, hushed words, short orders. Several archers tensed their bows and shot at Arnak's cue.

Unfortunately, the result was not what I had expected. Only one Spaniard fell on the spot, barely uttering a soft groan. The other, however, seeing what was happening, sprang up to flee. He received two arrows, but as we later saw, neither was fatal. He was now rushing wildly for the cover of the forest on the other side and screaming like a man possessed.

He understood the danger and guessed the proximity of an armed enemy. If he managed to warn his companions of what he had just learned, it could be our undoing. Everything hung on that one moment: whether the fugitive reached the forest.

He thumped across the clearing in great leaps. I quickly put my gun to my shoulder and took aim. Though it was night, the moon was bright, and I saw him as clearly as daylight. I put my whole soul into the accuracy of my eye. I saw his back jumping, sometimes above the front sight, sometimes below. He was fifty paces from us, sixty. How much was left to the brush? Fifteen leaps, ten?

I held my breath. I followed him with my sight as he bounded up and down, now raising my barrel, now lowering it. When the fleeing man was at the highest point of his trajectory, and the sight square on his back, just below the left shoulder blade, I pulled the trigger. A thunder clap, a fountain of fire, a kick of the musket butt in the shoulder. Through the flash, I saw his arms shoot up, but then the gunpowder smoke obscured my view.

"He's down!" I heard Arnak whisper. "You took him down!"

The thunderclap of the shot passed, my ears stopped ringing, and slowly the smoke dissipated. Now I saw him, too. He wasn't moving: he was dead. He lay only a few steps from the dark wall of the forest on the opposite side of the clearing.

"Did your shot not betray us?" Arnak asked, worried.

"I think not. If the Spaniards heard it, they would not know it had come from us. They would think it was one of their guns," I reassured him.

"But the Spaniard screamed!"

"Ah, yes, he did scream, which is substantially worse! Let us hope they didn't hear him."

"They had to hear him! He yelled like the devil!" Arnak said.

"Yes, but maybe they didn't hear clearly *what* he yelled. Until they see us, they won't know what he meant."

"Three down," chuckled Arnak. "These three may have seen us, but it doesn't matter now."

"Exactly! This is our advantage!"

After my shot, a profound silence fell in the glade, and nothing seemed to move in the thicket on the other side. The quiet seemed eerie, but there was nothing unnatural about it: we could hear dogs barking in the distance and even people's voices, but it all sounded quite far away, maybe half a mile away, maybe more. Apparently, the main chase had gone in the opposite direction, away from us.

Remaining hidden from the enemy was indeed our great advantage, and we had to preserve it for as long as possible. The corpses lying in the clearing and the traces of the skirmish could betray us. They had to be removed. The thing was, I didn't trust the silence; what if the enemy stood hiding in the forest on the other side? I talked to Manauri and the guys. They were all eager to move.

"Look through the spyglass! See if you can see something."

In the spyglass, the shadow of the thicket on the other side was no longer one shapeless blur but resolved into lighter and darker blotches and streaks. There was no wind, and the foliage was perfectly still. The forest hid an inscrutable secret, hatched some secret menace. Our fate was ripening within its depths—but the edge of it seemed safe at the moment. I didn't see anything suspicious.

"Let's move!"

Manauri and Arnak assigned tasks to individual men: to fetch the corpses, to collect the arrows and guns, to watch over security with bows ready.

I cleaned and loaded my gun and took my position among the shooters.

"Should we bring the dog, too?" asked Arnak.

"Of course!"

"Why don't we set up position on the other side of the clearing?" Vagura suggested.

"Why? To fall into their hands more easily? The clearing is our defense moat. It's safer for us here."

Manauri gave a signal, and the men jumped to it. There were no unpleasant surprises. They worked so briskly that no more than five minutes had elapsed since I had shot the Spaniard, and the clearing was empty again, as it had been for ages, and all the corpses lay hidden in the forest behind us.

And now, the edge of the thicket lay submerged in a great calm, broken only by the monotonous sawing of insects. It was a warm, moonlit night, with all the splendor of the tropics, and would have stimulated a gentle reverie, if the smell of blood and the occasional barking of the dogs did not disturb the peace of the absurd idyll.

# The Damned Dogs Again

Dawn was still far away. Sparse, puffy clouds appeared in the sky, covering the moon from time to time, each time causing near-total darkness. After the excitement of the skirmish, there came a moment of relative calm.

Taking advantage of the respite, I turned to Manauri, as usual, through Arnak:

"Where is the woman?"

The Indian pointed with his chin.

"Far away?" I asked.

"No."

"Is the conscious? Can she talk?"

"No clue."

"Let's go see her."

We took Arnak with us, leaving the men at the edge of the clearing under the command of Vagura, instructing them to be especially vigilant during our absence.

"A hundred paces from here," explained Manauri.

As we walked, Arnak asked about my plans.

"Plans?" I said. "Nothing has changed."

"So what do we do?"

"We will go to Mateo's rescue."

"Then we will go? We will not stay at the clearing?"

"No, we won't! But first, we must talk to the woman. Maybe she has something useful to tell us.

The African woman was sitting on the ground, her back against the trunk of a tree. When she heard our footsteps, she abruptly rose as if to flee. But having seen us, she immediately calmed down.

"Dolores! How are you?" Manauri greeted her in Spanish. "Are you hurt?"

"Not very much."

"Did my men give you something to eat?"

"Yes."

Then, seeing me, she began to tremble like a newborn calf.

"Calm down, silly girl!" Manauri said genially. "This is our friend. He will help us save Mateo."

"Mateo has been killed," whispered the woman.

"What? Are you sure?"

"Yes, I am sure. I saw how they stabbed him."

"Where did it happen?"

"Over there..."

She stopped, unable to speak further. Memories of the terrible event overwhelmed her. Manauri shook her shoulders gently, urging her to control herself and not waste our time.

Dolores was about thirty, the Indian assured me, but she looked fifty: years of captivity had worn her out. Abducted from Africa as a child, she spoke only Spanish. The Spaniards gave her a new name and a new language, burdened her with heavy labor, and destroyed her youth and health.

She soon regained self-control and began to answer us more

coherently. The events, the best we were able to reconstruct them according to her story, had gone like this: Mateo and his group, following our advice, camped near Turtle Point. On the last evening, their fire was burning near the shore as usual, and about an hour after sunset, they all went to sleep. No one noticed the ship, which must have appeared on the horizon at dusk, but the Spaniards easily spotted the light of the fire. They landed somewhere near the headland and approached the sleepers silently. However, one of their dogs whined prematurely and alerted the camp. Before the attackers closed in, the people in the camp jumped up and fled for the bushes. Women with small children were the worst off. In an effort to delay Spanish pursuit, Mateo, with three or four companions, faced the attackers and took all their momentum on himself. The defenders had only clubs and javelins; against them were the enraged dogs and all the power of the Spaniards with rapiers, spears, and rifles.

Mateo and the companions defended themselves fiercely for a long time—apparently, the enemy wanted to capture them alive, and therefore, they did not shoot—and before Mateo's men succumbed, the rest of the group managed to disperse into the forest. Dolores lost sight of her people early on and ran alone, without any idea where to hide. They shot at her twice but missed. They gave chase, and she managed to shake them. At last, she reached the clearing, where the dog overtook her, and we came to her rescue.

"How do you know Mateo is dead?" I asked.

"The Spaniards attacked him! When I looked back, I saw that he was surrounded."

"They may have wounded him but not killed him. They seem to want to take you all alive."

But Dolores was firmly convinced of Mateo's death and that of the three or four companions who had fought at his side, even though she had no clear evidence for it.

"Spaniards live off living slaves, not dead ones," Manauri remarked.

Arnak made an impatient wave of his hand and said:

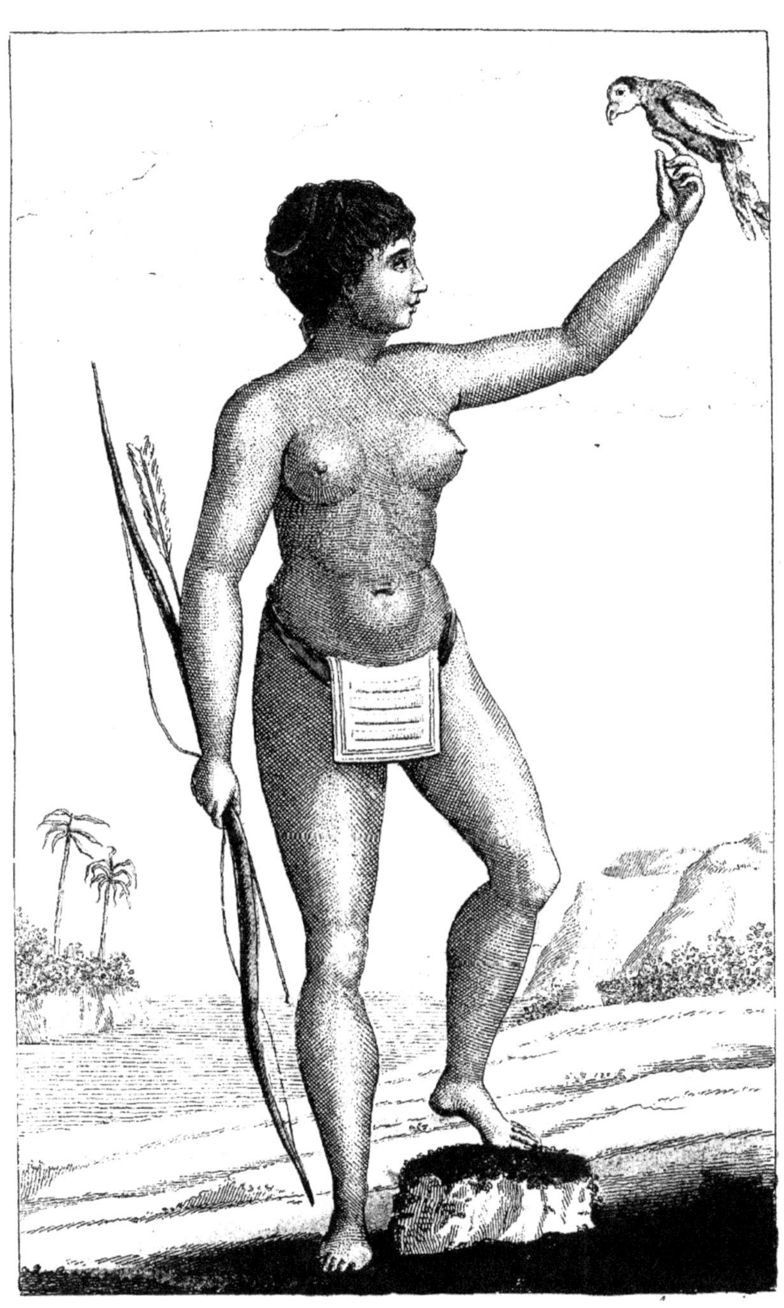

An Arawak Woman

"Until I see proof that he has been killed, I will assume Mateo is alive!"

Every one of us wanted Mateo to be alive, and contrary to all evidence, we refused to believe in his death. The stubborn giant enjoyed great popularity.

"Regardless of whether Mateo is dead or alive," I said, "his conduct during the attack and his decision to sacrifice himself to give others time to flee shows the man is a true hero."

"Mateo has a brave heart," said Manauri.

We heard someone approach: we saw the vague outlines of an approaching man.

"He's one of us," Arnak whispered.

It was one of the Indians watching at the edge of the clearing. He brought news. Arnak hastily translated it for me:

"Some people crossed the clearing and are on our side."

"Where?"

"He says a bowshot to the right. Over there, towards the center of the island."

"Spanish? Did they have dogs?"

"No dogs."

"How many?"

"Four, five."

"Oh!"

This was potentially frightening news: we had the enemy in front of us and someone who should also be considered the enemy—behind us. Those four or five in our rear could be real trouble. They had to be dealt with as soon as possible, even using firearms.

We returned quickly to our group, and I gave instructions: Manauri and his men were to remain behind and defend the clearing, while Arnak and Vagura and their men would follow me. We left behind the long-barreled muskets, useless in the thicket, and replaced them with fowling pieces loaded with lead shot. Even so, bows, spears, and knives—three excellent Spanish cutlasses had fallen into our hands—remained our weapons of choice.

"Ready?"

"Ready!"

We had a difficult task. The enemy was in the thick of the jungle, somewhere not far ahead of us, maybe only a few hundred paces, but we did not know where. We had to assume he was as vigilant as we were, straining his eyes and ears, and yet we had to first approach him and then surprise him so cleverly that none would get out of the fight alive.

At first, we walked along the edge of the clearing. A cloud covered the moon, which was good for us. We were all eyes and ears. The silence in front of us was complete, not a sign of the enemy.

After walking about two hundred paces, Arnak, who as always led the way, stopped abruptly. He raised his hand in a warning, listening. We heard the barking of a dog. It came from the other side of the clearing, where the five people had come from. Soon, we heard the cracking of breaking branches. There was no doubt: it was a dog—no, two dogs—bounding through the bushes, following in the footsteps of the people who had crossed the clearing before them.

"They are chasing the men!" whispered Vagura.

The dogs gave short, snarling barks, the sort you hear from hounds on a fresh trail of game. As they ran across the clearing, maybe two hundred paces from us, they had their noses on the ground.

"Yes, they're chasing them!" I said.

The two dogs were upwind and did not scent us. They crossed the clearing and fell into the forest on our side. Soon, we heard loud barking.

"They've caught them!"

"The Africans! The dogs caught them!" said Arnak.

"Let's go save them!" whispered Vagura.

"Wait!" I stopped him. "Men will follow the dogs."

"What to do?"

"Arnak! You and your men take cover on this side of the clearing, just where the dogs ran in. And make sure no one crosses the clearing alive."

"They're as good as dead! Can we shoot our guns?"

"Yes, but only in the last resort! First, only bows!"

"Yes!"

The dogs barked on furiously.

"Vagura, you and your people, follow me!"

We jumped to it, barrelling through the thicket, not caring about the noise. We went straight for the barking of the dogs.

"They'll tear them apart before we get there!" shouted Vagura as we raced.

"Look out, guys! No guns! No guns!" I shouted back.

There were seven of us. We could not miss them: the hounds showed us the way, and there they were: the Africans stood in a compact group, with their backs pressed against the trunk of a squat tree, and they fended off the enraged animals with sticks.

We got to within a dozen paces from them, and no one noticed us yet. The fight completely absorbed the attention of the people and the animals. Seeing that there was no imminent danger of attack, my Indians calmly took their positions. They surrounded the combatants in a semicircle only ten paces apart. It was all about not hitting the people under the tree by accident.

When all were ready, Vagura gave the signal.

The dogs, as if struck by lightning, fell silent and froze in motion. They were great, powerful dogs, Great Danes, stronger than the wolves of my Virginia woods. One of them, seeing a new enemy, turned to pounce on the nearest Indian, but three shots—in the face, in the neck, and in the chest—took him down on the spot. The other dog turned and tried to run away. But he ran into the last Indian in the semicircle. Struck in the head with a club and stunned, it took two arrows in the side and fell dead.

"Beautiful work!" I exclaimed with elation.

Just imagine the astonishment and shock of the Africans when, instead of the Spaniards, Indian defenders appeared before them! There were five of them: three Africans and that young Indian woman I had seen before: Mateo's wife. In her arms, she held her son, who was screaming at the top of his voice.

"He's yelling," I said with joy. "It means he is alive! But I beg you, calm him down!"

The moon had been shining for some time, and we could see quite clearly. I went to the Indian woman and gave her some fruit for the baby to calm the child up. Again, I was struck by her extraordinary beauty, her features full of sweet grace despite all her suffering and exhaustion. When I looked more closely at the child, I almost cried out in fright: his face was dripping with blood. No wonder it cried so much.

"What happened to him? Is he injured?"

"Yes, on the forehead."

The child had a deep gush on his forehead, and it was bleeding profusely.

"What happened?"

"A thorn in the bush, as we ran..."

Fortunately, I was wearing a shirt—my trophy from the burning Spanish brigantine. Without thinking, I tore a sleeve off it, cut it into strips, and tied it around the child's head. I will say this with some boastfulness: I tied it skillfully, for I had learned that useful skill in the woods of Virginia.

The boy soon stopped crying, and when he was given fruit to suck, his little face brightened with satisfaction. I touched his chin with my finger, and he smiled.

"Can you see?" I glanced cheerfully at his mother. "He's not afraid of me!"

She smiled as if to say: "Neither am I."

"Where Mateo?" she asked in Spanish.

For a moment, I wondered how to reply. She looked keenly at me.

"Is he dead?"

"*No se*," I replied with a Spanish phrase I knew. "I don't know."

"Where is he?"

Vagura translated for us in Arawak:

"We don't know exactly. But he is a great hero."

"Why?"

"Mateo attacked the Spanish! To make your escape easier."

"And he died?"

"Nobody knows."

"Could he be alive?"

"Yes, probably. The Spanish want to take you all alive."

The woman groaned. The news filled her with horror, and I regretted my careless words. She clutched the baby tightly to her.

"They will torture him on death! Like his brother!" she whispered bitterly. I took her firmly by the arm.

"What is her name?" I asked Vagura.

"Lasana," replied the youth.

"Lasana!" I said emphatically. "You must trust us! We will not rest until we destroy the Spanish or die ourselves. If Mateo is alive, we will free him."

I wanted to send the two women and two of the men back to the camp near my cave and take the third with me as a guide. But they refused: all the Africans demanded arms: they wanted to fight, and even Lasana decided to stay with us. She asked to be given a bow: like all Indian women, she was a good archer. Her place was, she announced, where her fate was to be decided.

Her demeanor exuded great courage and determination. I instructed the two women to take cover in a copse by the sea and watch and warn us by hooting if anyone crossed the clearing that way. And I assigned the three Africans to Vargura's command.

# A Painful Setback

On our return to Manauri, we held a brief council with our new allies. Believing that flight offered the only hope of survival once the Spaniards attacked, the three Africans had fled the camp with the others. They had heard Mateo's cries, but they didn't understand that he was summoning them to stand and fight. It seemed to them that everyone scattered into the forest, and only the three of them and Lasana were still left in a group.

"How many dogs do the Spanish have?"

They didn't know but were sure it was more than three.

"Can you lead our group to your old camp, where you were attacked by the Spanish?"

"Yes!"

"Then let's go there! If Mateo is alive and they hold him tied up somewhere, that is probably where he is."

The Africans didn't know how to shoot. They had never handled bows or guns, but they said they were good javelin throwers, so I gave each a javelin and a club. The eldest, named Miguel, approached me with a perplexed expression and asked if he could ask something important.

"Let's hear it!"

"We three..." he pointed to himself and his two companions but hesitated, unsure how to proceed. "The three of us... You understand, sir!"

"No, I don't!"

"We are in a stupid position... We are not cowards!... Believe us!... We really are not cowards! We just did not understand Mateo's cries!"

"No one is blaming you," I assured him.

"But we feel ashamed that he died and we ran away."

"I understand. That's what happened, it was an accident, accidents happen, and there is no point dwelling on this now."

"We want to fix it."

"Fix it? How?"

"Stand and fight! Order us to do something important! Order us to do something dangerous!"

Now, it was my turn to look at the concerned Miguel and his companions with embarrassment. I was touched by that simple impulse of chivalry, which the long humiliation of captivity had not been able to eradicate. It reaffirmed my faith in humanity. It inspired my confidence in every human being, regardless of the color of their skin.

It was only a brief reflection in my mind, for there was no time to dwell on it in this tense moment. I quickly came to my senses and returned to reality.

"Send you on some dangerous mission?" I repeated Miguel's words. "Do you think it's safe here? Remember: you must speak quietly because we don't know if the enemy is not hiding behind the next bush! Here, each of us, without exception, must give his best!"

"But let us..."

"Miguel, every one of us will have the chance to stand out and prove himself! No one is safe here: this will be a fight to the death against a cruel, merciless enemy! If we are careless, we will all die. There was one among us who wanted to stand out: Raisuli. He endangered himself and us, and he died. The Spaniards shot him right in front of us."

"We will not be careless, sir!"

"Okay, Miguel! I understand. Then remember this: our first rule is not to show ourselves to the enemy. The Spaniards still don't know we're all here, numerous, organized, and armed."

Again, I entangled myself in needless talk. Enough of this conversation with Miguel: we had more important concerns!

Did the Spaniards really not guess that we were here yet? The dogs that had chased the Africans had suddenly fallen silent, yet the Spaniards who had surely followed them never appeared in the clearing. Three enemies have died at our hands in the last hour and as many dogs. Have they not noticed? Did these developments not raise their suspicions?

The forest had been silent for a while now. The barking of the dogs had completely stopped. It was hard to shake off the feeling that some ominous danger suddenly hung over us in this mysterious silence.

Then, an Indian from the right wing crawled up to us. He said he heard something suspicious on the other side of the clearing. It sounded like the whining of a dog kept on a leash, a dog impatiently straining forward.

"Are you sure?" Manauri gave him a hard, critical look.

"We all heard it!" assured us the Indian.

I put the spyglass to my eye. It was dark, the moon had hidden behind a cloud again. Nevertheless, I noticed a faint movement in the opposite bush, about a hundred paces to our right.

"Attention!" I whispered.

Barely had I finished when a crouched figure broke away from the shadows on the other side of the clearing and ran steadily across toward our side. I caught it in my spyglass. A glance was enough to recognize the runner by his clothes.

"A Spaniard!" I said to my comrades.

He crossed to our side alone. If there were more Spaniards on the other side, they must have sent him to scout out our side of the clearing.

"We must get rid of him immediately!" I whispered.

"I! I!" Miguel leaned toward me and whispered with great urgency. "I'll take him!"

"Very well," I agreed. "But not alone! The three of you go."

"Good!"

"Remember: he's their spy. He will not be easy to take. He will be watchful and well-armed!"

"We'll do our best!"

"And remember the rule: do everything in silence!"

After their departure, we remained at our current position,

watching the clearing intently to see if anyone else would cross again. Nobody showed up.

A choked, short wheeze to our right heralded the quiet drama in the bush. Soon, the Africans returned with beaming faces.

"Got him!" Miguel snorted boastfully and placed the captured gun and pistol and the bags of shot and powder on the ground in front of me like a tribute.

"You've done well! Thank you!" I said.

"But this is for me?" he asked, showing me a beautiful, double-edged dagger. I nodded to him in agreement.

"This is our fourth knife!" Vagura chuckled and spoke through Manauri to Miguel.

"You did make sure he was dead, no?"

At that moment, a sharp bark nearby pierced the air, grating our nerves. Two dogs jumped out of the thicket from the same place from which the Spanish scout had come. But the animals did not follow him but ran diagonally across the clearing, straight towards us. Apparently, they had sniffed us out a long time ago.

"Arrows! Poisoned arrows!" hissed Arnak to the Indians.

We were not hiding on the very edge of the clearing but, for greater safety, a dozen paces into the thicket. As soon as the dogs reached the first trees on our side, they announced with furious barking that they had found their game. Struck at once by many arrows, they yelped piteously and fell, but a few moments too late: we had been discovered.

And then I did something stupid, the first stupid thing on that mission. Realizing that the Spaniards had set their dogs on us to discover our location and that the animals had given them the exact indication of our whereabouts, I should have ordered an immediate retreat. I didn't. Instead, I ordered my men to retrieve their arrows by pulling them out of the dead dogs.

"Faster!" I pressed.

Suddenly, right in front of us, on the other side of the clearing, several brilliant flashes ripped the darkness asunder, and the sound of several shots shook the air. There were eight, maybe ten, almost simultaneous, almost in a volley. The trees among which we took shelter rustled in the hail of lead. The enemy shot at us with lead shot.

Lying on the ground as I was, I felt a sharp sting on my left shoulder blade. Luckily, the bullet went sideways, having only glanced me. But from right and left came the moans of my wounded comrades.

I expected the Spaniards to charge immediately after discharging their volley. But apparently, they didn't feel very confident. No one emerged from the gunpowder smoke on the other side of the clearing.

"We shoot our guns?" asked Vagura.

"No! Do not shoot! No way! Everyone! Quiet! Retreat a hundred paces from the clearing! Let the healthy take the wounded! Come on, be quick!"

It turned out that there were five wounded besides me, including one shot in the head. I judged his condition hopeless. He lost consciousness as we carried him back.

"What to do with the dogs? Arnak turned to me. "Take them with us?"

I decided to stick to the principle of not leaving any traces. The Spaniards could have guessed a lot, but the less they knew about us, the better. So far, they still didn't know who we were, how many of us there were, and what weapons we had.

After retreating about a hundred paces from the clearing, we stopped. We sent out scouts in three directions, and they all reported that no one had come from the other side. This worried me because it suggested that the Spaniards were secretly plotting something new. I ordered a general retreat.

Meanwhile, the wounded Indian died. We left him lying next to Raisuli and threw the corpses of the Spaniards and the dogs in the deepest bush, where the devil himself would not find them before daybreak. I dressed the wounded, including myself. One of them, unable to fight, we sent back to join the two women.

And now we walked towards the sea, led by scouts some fifty

paces ahead of us. There were sixteen of us now, and we had captured valuable weapons.

What comforted me the most at that moment was the fighting spirit of our people. The setback had not shaken them. They were eager to fight and take revenge. I recognized the spirit of born warriors, of men who had fought before.

# The Scent of Gunpowder and Blood

After reaching the seashore, we turned right, crossed to the other side of the clearing, and made our way along its edge toward the place where the Spaniards had been when they shot at us. But we didn't find them there. The thicket was empty.

"Where did they go?" Arnak wondered uneasily.

"No idea," I grumbled.

I summoned Miguel.

"Can you lead us back to your camp?" I asked.

"Yes."

"Can we get there without meeting any Spanish along the way?"

Miguel stopped to think. I prompted him:

"Maybe if we went through the woods nearest to the shore?"

"That could be the best," he decided.

We headed back to the coast. For better combat readiness, I ordered two of our units to move side by side, some fifty paces apart, while the third was to follow in reserve.

Soon, the right column, where I was, came upon a corpse lying in bushes. By the agreed sign—the three hisses—we stopped the whole procession. When the moon looked out from behind a cloud, we recognized a black woman, one of Mateo's people, apparently mauled by dogs and cut with something sharp. Nearby lay the corpses of three children, all equally hideously cut up.

I shuddered. I had only one word for this:

"Monsters!"

We all had one and the same thought: this was the fate that awaited us if the Spaniards managed to catch us.

It was a good half a mile from the clearing to the camp. We had covered more than half that distance when we noticed movement ahead: in great silence, several Spaniards made their way in the same direction as us. The moon was out, and we could see their figures clearly at about two hundred paces.

"Let's take them!" Vagura said.

"We are too close to the camp," I replied.

"We'll finish them in no time. Let's go!"

"Vagura, no! We will make a racket and alarm the others."

"Racket! Big deal! Let's go kill them!"

"What if the others show up before we finish these guys? No, we can't do it."

"Yes, we can!"

I guess the sight of the murdered woman and her children raised his ire, and he did not want to listen. Luckily, Manauri got wind of what was happening and had enough influence among his men to command obedience. He breathed a few weighty words into Vagura's ear, and the youth relented without a murmur, looking a little sheepish.

The Spaniards, meanwhile, disappeared from sight. Fearing an ambush, I sent two scouts after them while the rest of us changed tack, moving slightly closer to the shore. In this way, we were completely covered from the side of the sea, and our patrols protected us from the front, the left, and the rear.

When I looked to the right, to the east, I saw the sky brightening with a leaden glow, foreshadowing imminent dawn, even though the light within the forest was still unchanged. Suddenly, I realized that our fate would be decided within the next hour, and the test would begin within minutes. The day was rising calm, windless, and a mild surf barely lapped the shore. The moon shone like a silver dollar in the western sky.[1]

A dark shape caught our eye on the sea. It was the schooner anchored right in front of us, no more than two or three musket shots from the shore.

"Standing right in front of the camp," murmured Miguel.

We could hear the noises of the camp in front of us.

"I believe," said I to the African, "that the Spaniards have set up camp in the same place as you."

"Yes," he confirmed.

Despite the tension, I smiled contentedly to myself. The prudence of having stayed in hiding was bearing fruit: the enemy had no idea who he was up against and had not retreated to the schooner. The Spaniards had remained on land and were acting as casually as if it were a picnic.

As time pressed on and the stars in the sky dimmed, we had to hurry and make sure we did everything to ensure a successful outcome of the coming battle. First of all, it was necessary to know the exact location of the enemy, so putting down our guns, five of us went ahead to scout out the ground before us: Manauri, Arnak, Vagura, Miguel, and me.

The area was overgrown with thorny bushes, which, however, diminished as we approached the camp. The ground gradually became stony, and the closer to the sea, the more stunted the vegetation that covered it and the bigger the rocks and boulders. There weren't even any coconut palms, which otherwise grew everywhere on the island.

Mateo's camp lay in the open before us. There were still the remains of huts built by his men and overturned by the events of last night.

In the absence of cover, it was impossible to get closer than a

---

[1] The Dutch pioneered the use and the counting of money in silver dollars in the form of German-Dutch *reichsthalers* and native Dutch *leeuwendaalders* in modern-day New York in the 17th century.

hundred paces. The Spaniards who had marched ahead of us just a few minutes ago had just returned to camp, and the men were talking loudly, relating their experiences to the others. A meal was being cooked on the fire.

"How many are there? Let's count them," I said.

I counted eleven. Arnak said: twelve.

"I guess that's everyone," I whispered. "Four dead, sixteen in total. That's about as many as we've seen on the schooner."

"Is no one left on the ship?" asked Vagura.

"Someone probably is left on board. All the more reason to think that these are all the Spaniards on the island."

It was a good thing to know. In all likelihood, there was no one in the woods behind us.

"Do you see any dogs?"

"I don't see any. They must have had only five, and we killed them all."

The Spaniards were extremely animated. Unfortunately, we were too far away for Manauri to understand what they were arguing about. But their gestures were easy to understand. Some, agitated, said something about danger, but others did not believe them.

At last, several detached and walked aside.

We strained our eyes, and our hearts skipped a beat. There, at their feet, on the ground, lay people tied up like hogs. The Spaniards now hoisted one of them up.

"Mateo!" wheezed Miguel.

But Miguel was wrong. It was not Mateo but another man from his group.

The Spaniards appeared to question him. When he didn't answer, they dragged him closer to the fire.

A young man was sitting there. Distinguished by rich clothes, he was no doubt their commander, for they all addressed him with great respect. I studied him through the spyglass. He was a young man, perhaps not more than twenty, with a black, narrow mustache and a face so smooth and regular that, but for his facial hair, I might have taken him for a beautiful girl.

He rose and pulled a burning faggot out of the fire. With a cruel grin, which I would have never associated with such a beautiful face, he approached the African and began to burn him on his cheeks, his belly, and under his armpits.

I realized the danger that threatened us: the enemy wanted to force a confession out of the prisoner, and the prisoner may well tell him about us. If he did, we were doomed.

"No time to lose!" I put the spyglass away.

The comrades saw for themselves what was happening in the camp and understood the situation. Few words of explanation were necessary. The plan of action was obvious to all:

"Run back to the men! We'll surround the Spaniards to make sure that no one can get away into the forest! Arnak's men will be here with me. Over there, in the center, Manauri, at the far end, Vagura. We'll all hit them at the same time! When you hear me fire, begin!"

"Finally!" whispered Vagura and took off.

"Don't forget my guns!".

I was left alone with Miguel. The Spaniards continued to burn the poor Negro, yelling at him and punching him. Then, the young man ordered another prisoner to be brought in and tortured him even worse: he burnt his whole face.

That second man did not have as much endurance as the first. What he said to the Spaniards, we could not hear, but he was screaming and pleading.

I looked to my left: the Indians weren't in their positions yet! The world was turning grey; the boulders in front of us became prominent, and the bushes took on color. Until now, I had only seen the whites of Miguel's eyes against a completely black background. Now, his features became more and more distinct. The day was breaking!

Miguel muttered something in Spanish in desperate impatience under his breath. There, by the fire, the Spaniards surrounded the interrogated African in a dense crowd. There was silence among them: they listened to the words of the captive with wrapped attention.

If we all fired at them now with lead shot, I thought to myself, we could wipe out the whole gang with a single salvo.

The Spaniards must have learned some weighty news from the tortured man because they suddenly went all abuzz like a beehive stirred with a stick. Some sprang to their feet and ran for the guns set up in trestles nearby. Others began to argue about what to do. I was terrified at the thought that they would set off into the woods. Then, not only would we miss the chance of a quick victory, but might well lose our lives in in a running battle.

I heard a rustle behind us: it was Arnak and his men. I sighed a sigh of relief.

"Where's Vagura?" I blurted out.

"On his way to his position, like you told him."

"Ah!"

"Here are your two muskets and your fowling piece."

Vagura, to whom I assigned the position farthest down, needed some time to reach his destination. But seconds mattered now and could make all the difference between success and failure.

O, thank you, good Lord, for the blessed loquacity of Spaniards! Standing by the fire, they argued endlessly, waving their arms, expressed profound thoughts, debated alternative plans, and looked up into the sky as if waiting for full daylight. The sun was about to rise when I took aim at the beautiful young man—to try the shot for size. He looked pretty in my sights.

Had the Spaniards been experienced fighters from the Virginia frontier, they would have long ago taken up defensive positions or gone to attack the enemy, guns in hand. But the Spaniards, in their bottomless pride, could not comprehend that instead of cowed, unarmed slaves, they were up against a well-organized and well-armed enemy. They were dawdling.

"Is Vagura already in position? What do you think, Arnak?" I asked.

"Long since!"

These words were a sentence of death for the Spaniards. I was in the process of selecting my first mark—the shot which would give the signal for attack, when a sudden commotion arose in the camp. The Spaniards finally decided something, and those who had their weapons at the ready moved quickly to the left of us, towards Manauri's position.

"Arnak!" I whispered. "Scream your head off."

I took aim at the closest Spaniard, some eighty paces from us. Arnak's yell froze the Spaniards in place. It only took a second for the musket shot to hit the target. Before the smoke had a chance to spread, I saw the enemy fall.

And now, from all three sides came the roar of gunfire and the screams of the Indians. Reaching out for my second musket, I tried to take in the whole field.

Unfortunately, the Indian fire did not have the effect I had expected. Perhaps they had aimed poorly, or, more likely, the distance had been too great—I don't know the reason, but no one else seemed to get hit except the man I shot. There were perhaps a few slightly wounded with lead shot, but the rest of the Spaniards escaped unharmed.

After firing their guns, our men rushed like a hurricane straight at the enemy. The Spaniards had barely recovered from their first fright before they began firing. But they shot in panic, too hastily, and they mostly missed. Still, they hurt us. Two of our Indians fell. Then, the Spaniards threw away their rifles and reached for swords and pistols.

Arnak and his men jumped out of hiding. Like mad, I jumped behind him, barely managing to catch up. I grabbed him by the neck.

"Stop!" I boomed. "Stay here!"

"Why?" he shouted back with passion.

"Stay!"

He stopped, shocked by the severe expression in my eyes. There was no time to explain. I handed him my fowling piece.

"Take it!" I called. "It's loaded!"

I pointed to the battlefield.

"We stay here and watch! Make sure no Spanish gets away alive!"

"Oh!" shouted Arnak, comprehension lighting up his face.

The failure of our gunfire was now thoroughly made up for with our arrows. The bow was my comrades' national weapon: they nocked and shot repeatedly as they ran. And their bows decided the day.

With furious screams and unstoppable impetus, they charged at the enemy from all three sides. But they had no desire to impale themselves on the Spanish swords: they did not close in for melee. They came to a full stop at a distance of perhaps two dozen paces, avoiding hand-to-hand combat, and shot their bows with a speed I have never seen in my life and with deadly accuracy. Three Spaniards fell within the first ten seconds of the attack. The rest, seeing impending defeat, scattered. Some fled towards the sea, and we couldn't really stop them. The others tried to run into the forest—in vain. Arrows overtook them, warriors with clubs overtook them, and when they overtook them, they sliced with daggers, stabbed with javelins, smashed with clubs. Some of the fugitives, seeing the hopelessness of flight, turned enraged to stab their pursuers with their swords, but they soon perished: a victorious frenzy carried away our avengers. Nothing could resist their wrath.

The cries of the dying, the groans of the wounded, the blood-curdling yells of the combatants, the billowing smoke and dust that covered the field, the pungent smell of gunpowder and blood all created an indescribable confusion. A large Spaniard, unnoticed in the tumult, slipped out of the melee and ran as hard as he could towards the thicket. He was apparently uninjured, running at breakneck speed. Nobody was chasing him.

"Arnak!" I shouted to my friend, pointing. "Look!"

Arnak sprang forward in a few mighty strides, blocking the Spaniard's way. He was about forty paces away. He fired. He hit. The

Spaniard tumbled off his feet, kicking up a cloud of dust. The boy ran up to him. He gave me a sign from a distance that the job was done.

Another one tried to scamper, but before I could target him, Miguel leaped after him and threw his javelin. The javelin buried its nose deep in the man's back. He fell flat, but Miguel was already upon him with his club.

# Annihilation

Glad to have spared a musket shot, I waved my hand to Miguel to congratulate him on his victory, but the African had no time to rest. Excited, he pointed towards the sea and shouted:

"Over there! They're escaping!"

I remembered now that some of the Spaniards, fleeing from the arrows of the advancing Indians, had fled for the beach.

"After them!" yelled Miguel. "Don't let them get away!"

And he was the first to give chase. Others ran after him.

The fight in the camp was over. No Spaniard was left standing. Men went over the field of battle and finished off the wounded. They were not inclined to take prisoners.

Two men set about freeing the Africans, but the rest ran towards the sea. About two hundred paces from the camp, three Spaniards managed to pull their beached launch into the water. By the time we got to shore, they were already rowing out of range of our guns.

They rowed through the small cove that narrowed to a few dozen paces at the outlet to the sea. On one side of the outlet, there were steep rocks, and on the opposite side, the shore was flat and sandy.

Most of us, including myself, ran like mad for the rocks. We hoped to pepper them with shot from the precipice. Manauri, however, made a keen assessment of the situation and directed some of his Indians to the opposite, flat side of the strait in order to catch the boat between two fires.

The Spaniards were ahead of us by a long shot. They rowed like mad to reach the strait before we got there. At first, it seemed that they might succeed. But it was impossible to row in such a mad rush for long. Soon, they grew weaker, and the boat slowed down.

When the first Indians got to the rock, the Spaniards were just passing the strait about fifty paces from the shore. The first arrows whistled in the air. Two hot-tempered Indians jumped into the water to swim to the enemy. The arrows, I noticed as I ran, were within range.

Spaniards redoubled their desperate efforts. They tried to get away from the rocks where we stood and inadvertently approached the other side of the strait. Here, meanwhile, a fierce pursuit had already arrived: the warriors sent by Manauri.

Gunshots rang out. A Spaniard fired a pistol at the swimmers. One of the Indians on the sandy shore had a fowling piece that had not yet been discharged. He took careful aim and fired. There was rattle and havoc in the boat. The lead shot cut the oarsmen down like a scythe.

By the time I reached the rocks, the boat was already being pulled ashore. Three dead Spaniards lay at the bottom. One of them was the beautiful young man. But, when throwing the corpses out of the boat, we learned that the cunning young man was only slightly injured and just playing dead. The Indians discovered this and wanted to kill him immediately, but I strongly objected to it.

"Why are you defending him?" They jumped at me in anger. I interposed myself, covering his body with my own.

They grabbed me roughly by the arms and tried to pull me away.

"Arnak! Vagura! To me!" I roared for my guys.

Arnak jumped to in an instant, Vagura came just behind him.

A "Blessing" of European Civilization

"What's going on?"

Horror showed on Vagura's face.

Arnak shoved one of the men grabbing me so violently that he, letting off me, rolled like a drunk. Simultaneously, Arnak shouted harsh words in Arawak. He must have ordered them to respect their commander because, reluctantly, the men eased off. But they were not cowed and, pointing angrily at the young Spaniard, demanded his death.

"Why don't you want him killed?" Arnak turned to me.

"We need to question him first! We want to know what the people on Margarita are up to. Maybe they're planning a second expedition?"

"Ah! You are right! I didn't think about that! But then you will allow us to kill him?"

I realized that my new Indian friends probably fought just like my Virginian comrades did—they gave no quarter and took no prisoners.

"The devil take him. Afterward, do with him what you will."

Arnak explained my thinking to the Indians, but they, still hot with battle frenzy, did not want to listen. And now a far more important reason for their agitation and unruliness came to light: that young man turned out to be the son of their hated master on Margarita, Don Rodrigues, the man who had ordered his dogs to rip the brother of Matco apart. Like father, like son: the young man had already established a reputation for cruelty.

Fortunately, Manauri managed to calm the hotheads, promising that the Spaniard would be punished in time. Gradually, my Indians allowed themselves to be talked around. They bound his hands and feet and threw him back into the boat, and two men rowed him back to camp.

After the overwhelming emotions and the enormous effort of the last twenty-four hours, a great relief came over us. We all sensed a strange, giddy-headed weakness. At times, we could not believe that we had won a victory and that our fierce enemy no longer posed a threat. But it was enough to look at the camp where the decisive battle had taken place to bring us back to reality.

We were still standing on top of the rock and gazing at the schooner with clenched fists. It had long ago raised the anchor and unfurled the sails. The sun was rising, and the morning breeze had sprung up. A light gust billowed the sails, and the slender ship was gaining distance. There was no way to catch up with it using just the boats in the bay.

I looked at the schooner through the spyglass. I could see only two Spaniards on its deck, two, no more. They worked furiously, as if burnt with scalding water, one at the sails, the other at the rudder.

"The ship is leaving!" said Arnak grimly. "If we only had taken it, it would have been so easy to reach the mainland!"

"And two Spaniards got away."

I saw in their flight a cause for worry. I did not hide my thoughts from Arnak and Manauri:

"These two Spaniards will now go back to Margarita. They'll alert everyone there, and within a day or two, they will return here with a force big enough to finish us all in no time. There is only one hope for us."

"I know."

"Well?"

"We've got to go to the mainland right away."

"Exactly! We have four boats and two rafts and no time to lose."

Both my Indian allies were of the same opinion. Arnak eyes shone with a hard light.

"I understand one thing," he said grimly. "Our fight is not over."

"No, it isn't," I said quietly.

# The Schooner Again

Returning to the Spanish camp, we first released the Africans. There were three of them, badly mauled but alive; the fourth, unfortunately, was dead: Mateo. The Spaniards had terribly mutilated his body and broken his head open. He was barely recognizable. As I was expecting his wife to arrive at the camp at any moment, I had Mateo's body buried as soon as possible so as to spare the young woman the terrible sight.

Two Africans were missing. Manauri sent men into the forest to search the area, and indeed, their corpses soon turned up. And now we knew that we were not leaving anyone behind.

While the Indians prepared our three boats for departure—I wanted to use the boats to take our wounded back to our camp on the east coast of the island—I examined our captive in the presence of Manauri, Arnak, and Miguel. How much insolence, cynicism, and audacity was in that juvenile degenerate! To my factual questions, he answered only with curses and abuse. I was stunned that such a stream of abominations and spittle could come from such shapely lips.

His ferocity knew no bounds. When I pointed out to him that he should respond more politely to a man who, after all, saved him from certain death, he just snorted derisively. He seemed not to realize that his life hung in the balance.

"You must have gone mad!" I said calmly. "Look at the corpses of your comrades. You are about to join them."

"Well, yes, those are my men. But you know who I am."

"And who are you?"

"The son of the governor of Margarita! None of these slaves will dare to touch me! And you, filthy traitor of your race, will hang before anything happens to me!"

I felt a strong desire to slap the rascal in the face, but I restrained myself in time.

"So you think that a governor's son is untouchable?"

"Of course! You will want the ransom, won't you?"

What a strange face! Even in its hateful contortion, it lost little of its eerie charm. What a strange phenomenon: a hideous demon in the shell of an angel!

"You are mistaken," I said. "Your life hangs by a thread."

The young man laughed impudently.

"Another ship will be here tomorrow. You rabble will learn who your master is, and we will then see whose life hangs by a thread."

"What ship?"

"What ship? A ship from Margarita!"

"And why would another ship come here?"

"Are you blind? Didn't you see our schooner sail away? Where do you think it went? What do you think my father will do when he hears of our fight?"

So that was the basis for his self-confidence: on the one hand, the threat of the second ship, and on the other: his value to us as a hostage. Those were pretty good grounds for confidence, and he was probably guessing my plans for his future. For I was resolved to defend his life, even if all the Indians were to turn against me: defend it, of course, not for his beauty, but for our own safety. He was the son of a distinguished Spaniard. To hold him alive in our hand as a hostage might just turn out to be our trump card in the event of another invasion from Margarita. He could be the key to our freedom.

While we talked, suddenly, loud shouts reached us from the sea. Several Indians came running towards us.

"The ship! The ship!" they cried.

Speak about the devil, I thought: the second ship from Margarita was here! But it turned out not to be the case: on the contrary, the news was very good.

In the morning, at sunrise, there had been an offshore wind, but it lasted for no more than half an hour and then completely subsided, and the air became totally still. There were often such moments in the waters surrounding my island, but normally, they never lasted more than an hour or two, and by noon, there was always a strong onshore wind.

But this time, the schooner had not gone a mile before all wind stopped, its sails went limp, and it came to a standstill. The news of the ship's arrest suddenly raised the hope that we could still take her. We all grabbed our weapons and rushed for our boats like mad.

In the midst of the general fervor and bustle, we had to keep things straight. Having summoned Arnak, Vagura, and Manauri, I laid out my plan to them: we would take the two boats of Mateo's party. Arnak and I would position ourselves on the larger one, Vagura on the smaller one. All capable Indians and Africans would row except the three of us. Only the three of us would be shooting. We'd take all the long-range muskets, and to make them carry farther, we'd give them extra gunpowder and stuff half with bullets, the other half with lead shot.

"Should not the others bring their own weapons, too?" asked Vagura.

"They should bring their weapons, of course, but they must not interfere with our aiming and shooting. When we shoot, they must stop rowing and remain motionless and keep the boat as steady as possible."

"Yes, so that we can aim well!"

Manauri nodded his agreement and gave the appropriate commands. He assigned men to the boats and took the helm of the larger one. In the meantime, we loaded our muskets. We were going to fire first those about which we already knew that they carried well.

"Put a few men in the Spanish launch, too."

"Put any shooters in it?"

"No, no, it's just to confuse the Spanish."

Three men took the launch.

We took off. The men worked their oars very hard, tiny waves splashed against the boat. I stood at the bow, Arnak at the stern. After leaving the bay, we went out onto the open sea, which was as calm as a lake on a clear day. Here and there, the gentlest puff of the weakest of all breezes flaked the surface of the water, but each time, the wind died out almost immediately.

The schooner had dropped its anchor. Its sails hung down flaccidly.

As soon as the Spaniards saw us, they began to rush about the deck like mad, now moving the sails, now some other equipment. I could see through my spyglass that, at last, they set about loading their muskets.

We moved fast. The rowers worked furiously. Sweat poured from their bodies in rivulets. The morning cool was over, and the day was turning very hot. The men's prolonged captivity had undermined their energy and weakened their muscles. They were exhausted, but the awareness of the importance of our mission gave them unexpected energy.

We were within a quarter of a mile of the ship. The sea was still calm. There was no doubt that we would reach our goal and that the schooner would soon fall into our hands. The two Spaniards might inflict losses on us, yes. But the final victory had to be ours.

I glanced at Arnak and once again told him to remind the oarsmen of this rule: when it came to shooting, they were to pull the oars out of the water, take shelter in the bottom of the boat, and remain deathly still.

The schooner had an upraised bow to shield it from frontal waves, but the stern was low and unprotected. So we approached the ship from the side of the stern. The Spaniards, anticipating this maneuver, placed two chests at the stern to use as cover.

"Watch out!" I called to my friend. "I'll use a little trick, and maybe they'll fall for it."

"What trick?" Arnak asked.

"I'll shower them with shot from too far away." Maybe I'll panic them into firing, too. Then they will have no time to reload."

That trick used to work quite well in Virginia, so why not here? When fired upon, men often can't resist firing back.

At two hundred steps, I fired my musket, aiming high above the head of the enemy. We saw the shot buzz and pluck at the sails and rigging of the ship.

I grabbed my second musket, and I aimed it like I was going to shoot again. This provocation the excited Spaniards could not stand: they discharged their guns. Small surprise, they were not experienced soldiers—they were slave catchers. Their bullets came up short, as I had predicted: we saw them splash in the water in front of us.

"Now, row! Row! Row! Row like the devil!" I shouted to my Indians. "Hoo-hah! At them!"

A dozen hard pulls of the oars brought us within a good distance of the ship.

"Attention!" I called. "Everybody stop! I will shoot!"

"Me too?" Arnak asked eagerly.

"Only when you see a clear target!"

The oarsmen lay flat at the bottom of the boat, which continued to glide with its own momentum. She glided over the water as smoothly as a salt shaker over a dinner table, not a wobble to her body.

The Spaniards probably had only the two guns they had just fired because, hiding behind the crates, they were eagerly reloading them. They were sometimes visible—now the top of the head, now an elbow, now a foot, and even then only for the blink of an eye. No sooner had we aimed at something than it was out of sight. Though they were clearly in a huge hurry, they were careful not to expose themselves.

But then one of them showed more body than he should have. Before he could disappear behind the crate, I fired at him, aiming at the end of the spinal column. The trusty musket carried well, and the ball hit the target. A scream rang out. Wounded, unable to control himself, he uncovered his head. Another shot, this time from Arnak's gun, and the enemy slumped. I smiled at Arnak with admiration, this was some shooting!

Meanwhile, the second Spaniard, taking advantage of the confusion, fired. The scum fired lead shot. He aimed for me, apparently, but my neighbors got it. Although they were lying on the bottom of the boat, two got peppered. I assumed the lone Spaniard had no more guns to fire, so I ordered my men to row fast: we were going to board. But I was wrong: another shot came from the ship. Evidently, the Spaniard used the loaded rifle of his fallen comrade. Luckily, just as he exposed himself to aim and shoot, Vagura fired at him. The Spaniard panicked, and his shot went wide.

I had lost track of his guns. So, I preferred to go for the sure thing: keeping an eye on the schooner, we fired every time the enemy peeped even slightly from behind his chest. In this way, we completely pinned him down and hoped that either one of our bullets would get him or we would clamber aboard and take him hand-to-hand.

I don't know how long it took—us shooting again and again—when the end came from a completely different direction. Busy with the gunfight, we completely forgot about the Spanish launch and her three crew. Nobody paid any attention to them. They patiently circled the schooner at a healthy distance, and while we focused the attention of the Spaniard on us, they approached the schooner from the bow and climbed over the side. We were astonished and terrified to hear, out of the blue, the war cries of the three Indians as they rushed the lone Spaniard. They had bows and clubs, and they dealt with him in no time.

The schooner was ours.

Is it impossible to describe my joy, why—my intoxication!— so strange, so overpowering, as I stepped aboard the Spanish ship, realizing the full importance of the moment. I approached my faithful friends, Arnak, Vagura, Manauri, and the rest of the Indians, and shook their hands with emotion.

"We won! We won!" I kept muttering in a daze.

"The path home is clear!" said Arnak, looking at the southern horizon where the misty line of the mainland loomed.

"Yes, it is clear!"

Some of the Indians, trained in the art of seamanship during captivity, stayed on deck to bring the schooner closer to the camp when the wind returned, and the rest got into the three boats and rowed ashore.

# Judgment

When we entered the bay, Manauri gave me a sign that he would like to talk to me in private, only in the company of Arnak, who would serve as our interpreter. As soon as we came ashore, we walked to one side.

"The situation is now clear," began the chieftain. "There are no more obstacles before us. When would you like to leave the island?"

"The sooner the better. Two days?"

"And maybe even sooner? Are you not afraid of a new ship coming from Margarita?"

"Not immediately, no. But later, maybe in a few days or a week, yes, someone will come looking for these Spaniards."

"So, the quicker, the better?"

"Absolutely."

I looked at Manauri searchingly, for I couldn't understand why he called me aside to discuss our departure time. And then I guessed it. It was about the prisoner.

"You defended him before," said Manauri, looking into my eyes with a peculiar fierceness, "because you wanted to get information out of him. He insulted you and us and told us nothing. Do you think it will be different now, and he will say something?"

"We'd have to try it."

Manauri narrowed his eyes and shook his head with stubborn resolve.

"No, he won't tell us anything. Besides, what can he tell us? He knows no more about the timing of the relief party than we do. We will now kill him."

Manauri spoke with a firmness which I had never seen in him.

It seemed that last night's fight won another victory in addition to the victory in arms: it killed the slave in him, and freed the tribal chief.

I told him what I had been thinking—namely that the young Spaniard should be held hostage for as long as possible.

"A hostage?"

"Yes."

"Didn't you just say that we'd be leaving in two or three days, and the enemy was not expected before our departure?"

"As things are, we may yet be surprised, and a good chief anticipates all possibilities."

Generally, Manauri had a rather gentle, good-natured demeanor, but now his features hardened as if hewn from stone.

"Yes, Yan, but a good chief also listens carefully to his warriors. There is only one solution. Yan, we kill him."

"Don't you think it would be a kind of murder?"

"No, and I don't like this manner of talking."

"I didn't mean to offer you."

"I understand. But murder?" Manauri objected to the word. "You call administration of justice murder? No, we will not murder him. We will pass judgment on the prisoner. Anyone will be able to express their opinion, you too, if you wish to speak in his defense. But justice must be served."

And then he added with what I understood to be irony:

"You, whites, use courts to put criminals to death. We will do the same. The Spanish courts were not just, but ours will be."

I saw his point and reflected on my own attitude. Why did I stand up in defense of this hateful Spaniard, giving my companions in the process the impression that I had a special consideration for the monster? After all, I didn't want to defend him at all but had only thought that he was more useful to us alive than dead.

During the fight for the camp, two Indians and one African died. We buried them next to Mateo. We built a high mound of stones over their grave, thus paying homage to them and to their extraordinary African commander. I put a lot of effort into this work myself, wishing to demonstrate to all that I held no grudge against Mateo. His legitimate distrust of white people had been well justified.

At sunrise, a stiff wind arose. By noon, the schooner arrived at the entrance of the bay and dropped anchor and all our people—except three sentries left on the schooner—assembled in the camp. Manauri immediately ordered the prisoner's trial.

Near the camp stood a solitary tree, and we all sat in its shade. Next to me, on each side, sat the boys, Arnak and Vagura. The bound Spaniard was brought before us. The haughty youth, sensing what was about to happen, lost his former hardiness, and there was no more verbal abuse from him. He was silent and grim.

Manauri briefly recounted several of his crimes against the slaves on Margarita and demanded that those present express their opinion as to his fate. Everyone, without exception, the unscathed and the wounded, men and women (there were two of them, Dolores and Mateo's widow, Lasana)—declared unanimously in favor of the Spaniard's death.

Then Manauri looked at me and asked me to speak.

"What's my opinion?" I said. "Everyone has spoken, and all think the man deserves death. My opinion is not needed."

Manauri responded:

"You are mistaken. Your opinion matters to all of us."

"I do not see why."

"Because, Yan, we owe this victory over the Spaniards to you. Because we value your bravery and your prudence. Because you are our companion and our friend. And also, because you are of the same race as him, so you will understand him best."

"What do you wish to hear from me?"

"We want you to tell us whether this man deserves death or not."

"He deserves death," I said without hesitation.

When Arnak translated my answer, a general whoop of approval went up. But I raised my hand and said that I had more to say.

"Speak up!"

"The Spaniard deserves to die, and we will kill him. But we should not kill him now, not yet, not here."

"Then when?"

"I think we should execute him after we have reached your native village."

At these words, a veritable hurricane of opposition rose up. No, no, no! My companions demanded his immediate death. Such was the hatred in their hearts; so much hurt and bile had accumulated in them that they did not want to hear the voice of reason and angrily rejected any possibility of keeping the man alive. I realized that this storm could not be tamed. The matter of the prisoner's immediate death was a foregone conclusion.

With every sign of reluctance, I expressed assent.

Scarcely had the people calmed down when a new disagreement broke out concerning the kind of death the condemned should die. Many demanded various elaborate tortures, but in the end, most agreed to have the Spaniard buried alive in an anthill to be slowly eaten alive by ants.

Manauri cast an uneasy glance at me, and seeing me turn pale, he said:

"Listen up, people!" he raised his voice. "We must find another death for him!"

"Why? Anthill the man! Anthill him!"

"No," Manauri said. "Death in an anthill takes days, and we don't have time. We have to leave the island as soon as possible."

The idea of the anthill was abandoned because the chief's argument convinced everyone: it was impossible to sail away before ascertaining the death of the Spaniard, and the anthill would take too long. So again, a discussion followed on the kind of torture to be employed, but by then, I had had enough of the talk. I jumped to my feet and yelled:

"No, no, no! We will not torture him! There will be no torment! When a hero has to kill, he kills, but he does not torture. Let us just kill the Spaniard!"

What a storm broke out now! How the people's eyes flashed with anger! But I got on my high horse and would not yield an inch. I have never seen the famous traditional Indian tortures of my part of the New World, but I have heard of them. And I have seen men tortured during our rebellion in Virginia, and I did not want to see it again. When the shouting quieted down a bit, I spoke:

"I demand that you act like honest, honorable men. Only degenerate beasts like the Spanish abuse the defenseless! If you want to be my friends, I ask you to behave like proud and honorable men. If you want me to be friends with you, be honest warriors! Be wise! Consider what I am saying! That's my last word."

The two boys and Manauri spoke in my support, but a few fierce enthusiasts stood their ground and incited others against us. I had put the matter on a knife's edge: the consequences could be disastrous for me.

But then there was a new development. A woman asked to speak. The young Indian woman—Mateo's widow—came closer to me and, pointing in my direction, began to speak to them in Arawak and Spanish. Her calm composure made a strong impression, and her deep and strong voice seemed to me like she was singing.

"What is she saying?" I whispered to Arnak.

"That she is on your side. That she is Mateo's widow, and she demands that we listen to you. That... er... hohoho!"

"'Hohoho' what?" I asked impatiently.

"My goodness, what are we learning about you!"

Arnak gave me a sidelong look, and his typical ironic sneer flickered on his face.

"I didn't know this about you," said Vagura with a grave expression.

"What is it? Will you tell me, you rascals?"

"She says that you are a great man. That friendship with such an exceptional man has to be appreciated. That..."

I was pretty sure they were mocking me.

But whatever the case, the words of the Indian woman made a strong impression on her listeners and overcame the resistance of the would-be torturers. Grateful to the woman, I thanked her with a glance and a smile.

After that, everything went quickly and easily. We decided to hang the Spaniard from the same tree under which his trial had been held. The bindings at his feet were cut, he was led under a branch, and a rope of liana was thrown around his neck.

His eyes flashed with fear, he seemed to want to shout something. When he hanged, and his convulsions stopped, a hideous change came over his beautiful face: his features, so beautiful and alluring, after death became imbued with a repugnant expression of cruelty, a feeling that evidently permeated his hideous being when he was alive.

The scene was disturbing, but I understood its meaning like this: this was not an act of revenge of twenty or so wronged Indians and Africans, but the legitimate act of justice and self-defense of the oppressed.

# The Question of Identity

After the execution, we transferred our wounded from the camp to the schooner and set out south along the shore. We had a gentle northerly wind, so when we sailed east, we had it first to port and then head on. The schooner was agile and maneuverable, her sails were well set, and she tacked beautifully into the wind. We had tied our three boats to her stern.

In the afternoon, we came into the vicinity of my camp and anchored a quarter of a mile from shore, just opposite my hill. Everything was fine in the cave. The women were glad of our victorious return and promptly prepared a feast for us and tended the wounded.

I summoned all the unscathed to a council and asked them again when we should leave the island.

"The earliest we can," replied Manauri. "Tomorrow morning if we can!"

"Very well, let us leave tomorrow morning! We still have three hours until sunset, and we have work to do!"

First of all, our corn had to be harvested. It is true that we found a good supply of provisions on the schooner, but it would be a pity to abandon so much ripe corn, which we had guarded for so many weeks.

We all set about harvesting and soon filled a dozen baskets with the golden cobs.

We now had four boats and two rafts, a veritable fleet of vessels. But what to do with the largest boat, which, being heavy, would be too heavy to haul? We decided not to destroy it but to hide it from the elements for some possible future use: drag it into the cave and seal it behind a wall of stones.

We moved the boat to the cave. By the time we had accomplished that task in the sweat of our brow, the daylight had not yet faded. I came up with the idea of leaving a memento of my stay on the island and carving my name on the side of the boat. As I carved my name, a powerful emotion welled up in me. I looked with profound feeling at my hunting knife, the only keepsake I had of the old days in Virginia, and holding in my hand the jagged, worn, dear instrument, I thought of the great merit of this faithful friend. How many times had I owed my life to it during the hard times of my first period on the island!

Using this beloved instrument, I carved on the broadside of the boat:


JOHN BOBER


I looked at my handiwork and winced: why "John"? Why not

"Yan"?

But it had already happened, it could not be undone, so below I added the word:

POLONUS[2]

And under the name, I carved the date:

AD 1726

During supper, Manauri solemnly asked us for a moment's attention. Addressing the Africans, he expressed his doubt about whether, living alone on the mainland, they could survive and not fall again into the hands of the Spanish. Therefore, he offered them not only hospitality and protection in the Indian village but also an adoption into the Arawak tribe on equal terms with the others. The Africans received his words with gratitude.

Then Manauri turned to me and assured me that the tribe would give me all the help I needed to get safely to the English-inhabited islands near the Orinoco River. Then he added:

"But if I have to speak from my heart, we would prefer that you stay with us for as long as possible and even for life! With us, you will never lack friendship, respect, or food, Yan!"

I thanked him for his kind words and for his invitation. I did not have the heart to avow my refusal.

On the last day of our stay on the island, we woke up long before dawn and began to transport all our possessions and supplies to the schooner. I decided to donate my firearms to the Indians on our arrival in their ancestral village, and I took particular care to ensure that they

---

[2] POLONUS (*Latin*): A Pole, a Polish Man

were not damaged and remained in good condition. We had nearly thirty long guns and a great supply of gunpowder and lead: firepower which, properly used, could assure the survival and freedom of the Arawaks for many, many years to come. I entrusted Arnak and Vagura—best aware of the importance of these weapons, as they were—with the custody of the guns.

We didn't raise the anchor until around noon when a stronger wind arose. We headed straight east for as long as possible, sailing parallel to the mainland but just north of where the black belt of the current shone on the sea. There were thirty of us: eleven, including one woman and three children, had lost their lives during the Spanish attack. We had paid a high price for our freedom.

Arnak, Vagura, and I stood on the ship, leaning against the side, staring at the receding island—Robinson's Island, as I once called it.

We had spent over four hundred days on it, toilsome and tense days; days of dogged struggle against nature, animals, and men; days full of hard work, tension, and ardor, sometimes even doubt. It had been a long, exhausting, but victorious path through the tangle of events as intricate and thorny as the vegetation of the island. But had I traveled that path in vain? Was my struggle without consequence? Was my survival the only reward for the experience?

Oh, no!

Saying goodbye to the palm trees slowly sinking in the blue haze, following with my eyes my hill fading in the distance, the hill from which I had so often looked for help and salvation; I did not curse the island for having held me a prisoner for so long. I did not curse it, for I was leaving it richer and happier than I had found it. On a deserted island, strangely enough, I discovered a great treasure: I discovered man in myself and man in my neighbor. There, the scales fell off my eyes, opening my sight to a people of another race. There, I enriched my heart with the experience of new friendships.

No! I did not curse that uninhabited island.

Someone silently approached us and stood next to me. It was

Lasana. She held the baby in one arm and rested the other hand on the railing next to mine. She looked at the island for a moment, then turned her gaze at me. It seemed to me that I read warmth in her big black eyes.

I put my hand on top of hers. She did not withdraw it.

# A Meeting at Sea

For two whole days after we left the island, we sailed steadily eastward, each morning seeing the sun's red disc straight ahead as it emerged from the ocean. The ocean was completely empty. We saw no ship, no boat, no sail as far as the eye could see and were very encouraged by this loneliness. The wind and waves came from the northeast, and though unskilled hands spread the sails and the clashing sea currents made our navigation difficult, our schooner was not a slouch, and she made good progress. Throughout the first and second day, we never lost sight of the mainland to the south of us, for this part of South America was hilly. Chief Manauri and his Indians strained their eyes, searching for a familiar peak, under which, they told me, their villages lay. It was called the Mountain of Vultures.

"But will you recognize it from this far away?" I wondered. "The land is so far! And every mountain looks pretty much like another."

"We will know, we will know," answered Manauri in Arawak, and Arnak and Vagura translated his words.

"Maybe we should take the ship closer to the shore?" I suggested.

"There's no need to! There may be underwater rocks closer to shore, and we will recognize our mountain from far away because it looks very distinctive."

How eagerly we watched for that mountain, the herald of

better days! Over there, in the Arawak villages, our long journey to freedom would finally come to an end. There, my Indian friends would be among their own again.

And I? Would I be able to reach the English islands from there? Would my Indian friends help me, as they had promised? I sensed that they would not let me down. The experiences of the last week have bound us with a lasting friendship.

Fate continued to be kind to us. The sea was empty, the weather clear, the winds favorable. When the second evening came, I ordered the sails taken in so as not to run into anything in the dark. I entrusted Manauri and Arnak with the night watch. The night passed peacefully, without incident. But at dawn on the third day, a great cry arose on the deck.

"Spaniards! Spaniards!" the ominous cry pierced the air. "They're chasing us! They're behind us! Run! Run!"

All jumped up, suddenly wide awake, and I dashed, pell-mell, for the helm. Arnak was there: it was his watch.

"Over there! Over there!" he cried out, pointing north with his hand.

Everyone stared north, their faces ashen with fear. The night was dying; the sky had paled; already, the glow of the coming day lit the sea and all the objects on it. In the distance loomed the outlines of a phantom. Yes, it was a ship: a great three-masted brigantine. In the still-reigning dusk, she seemed imposing, powerful, menacingly magnified by the morning air. She was on the same course as we, due east, only farther out to sea, distant from us, as far as we could judge it in the twilight, about three-quarters of a mile as the crow flies, perhaps a bit less.

"Make all sail!" I shouted and took the wheel out of Arnak's hands. The youth translated my command. Having lived on a ship, he knew what had to be done, and our men got busy.

"Arnak! You stay by me! I will need an interpreter on hand!"

As a gang, we were the world's poorest excuse for sailors: I, their helmsman, have served but a few months on a privateer, mostly scrubbing decks and learning how to fire a cannon. But the Indians, a coast people, were familiar with the sea and were thus quick to grasp the purpose of the rigging once it was explained to them.

The sails went up and unfurled in all their glory. The ship suddenly took on speed. The water at our sides gurgled louder. When I turned her more toward the land, to move away from the brigantine, the wind, hitherto blowing aport, now turned more afore, and this gave us even more speed.

"Do they know who we are? You think?" asked Arnak, keeping a close eye on the brigantine.

"I guess not. It's not light enough. Besides, look, the brigantine is still following its old course."

"Maybe they are not chasing us, after all?"

"Maybe. Maybe they've just happened this way."

"Are they Spaniards? Someone else?"

"Get me my spyglass! On the double!"

The men, having put up the sails, now congregated near me, all staring at the brigantine."

"You're going ashore?" asked Manauri anxiously.

"No, just trying to put a little more distance between us and them," I explained.

"The sea is dangerous here. Many underwater rocks."

"We don't have much of a choice. We have to try our luck. Manauri, take a few men afore, stand at the prow, and watch the surface of the sea. If you see anything—rocks, shoals, you yell."

Several men took positions at the prow.

I could not tell through the spyglass whether the brigantine was Spanish. When the day broke, she discovered us, and immediately turned towards us. Was it mere curiosity that motivated them, or was it really the pursuit from Margarita? Or perhaps they had only noticed our change of course and decided to see why we were fleeing? Whatever the case, we had to avoid them like the plague.

The turning of the brigantine naturally caused a stir on board. The intention of the Spaniards became apparent: they wanted to close in to take a look. And this could mean disaster. The Indians and Africans standing around me looked at me with panic as if seeking help or encouragement.

"Never fear!" I called out in a loud voice. "They will never catch us!"

"How can you be so sure?" asked Manauri.

"Brigantines have a deeper draft. That's why I took our schooner closer to shore because she will not dare follow us here, among the shoals."

"And if she does?"

"Then we will abandon ship and flee ashore. But it won't come to this. Look! We are faster than she is. We are leaving her behind."

Our schooner was long and narrow, shaped like a swift pike, while the brigantine was squat and stocky, shaped more like a turtle. And indeed, it didn't take much discernment to see that the gap between our two ships was steadily increasing, even as we turned east and resumed our original easterly course parallel to the shore again.

Suddenly, there was a whistle in the air, and a cannonball kicked up a fountain of water about a musket shot away to our starboard. A moment later, we heard the dull report of a gunshot from the direction of the brigantine: the Spaniards had fired at us. Dolores, the African woman whose mind had become a little unhinged after her near-death experience on the island, began to scream. And she kept it up until Lasana embraced her tenderly and hushed her like a child.

"Arnak!" I said loud but clear and calm so that everyone might see my composure. "Take a few friends and bring all our weapons on the deck: muskets, fowling pieces, blunderbusses, pistols. And all the sabers and pikes. Then load all the guns."

Arnak immediately translated my words into Arawak.

And then something happened, something seemingly minor but so surprising that I was astonished by the discovery. What happened was this: one of the Indians addressed by Arnak asked him:

"And the gunpowder, too?"

"Yes!" replied my friend.

"And the bullets?"

"Of course!"

But the Indian, a little slow apparently, somehow did not understand clearly and was asking something about the powder. Since I worried about every passing minute, I lost my patience with the dawdling, bypassed Arnak, and spoke directly to the Indian:

"Go bring everything!"

"We will shoot?" asked the Indian.

"I don't know! Bring everything!"

And the point of my discovery was this: I blurted it all out in... Arawak. I am sure I mangled the language, got all the grammar wrong, and probably mispronounced it, too, but I understood their conversation, spoke in their language, and was, in turn—understood. So I, a Virginian, an Englishman of Polish descent—spoke Arawak! How did that happen?

The second of the brigantine's cannonballs hit the sea, this time much closer to our ship, but even that was unable to suppress my astonishment: until that very moment, I had not realized that I had been learning Arawak, unconsciously, unawares. How did that happen?

There was no magic to it, I suppose: the explanation was all too simple. During my year of cohabitation with Arnak and Vagura on Robinson Island, we always spoke English since both boys were pretty good at it. But when the two Indians talked to each other, they used Arawak, and they were never embarrassed to use it in my presence.

And I listened to the sound of their tongue unwittingly and heard so much of it that, without realizing it, I must have learned individual words and even whole phrases. I paid little attention to all this, so I acquired this peculiar skill imperceptibly, in the background, under the surface, as it were, and now, in a moment of need, this ability suddenly surfaced up, revealing itself fully, springing like Athena out of the head of Zeus. In the general tension, no one on the schooner noticed it—no one, that is, except myself. To them, speaking Arawak was the most obvious thing on earth.

Meanwhile, people brought weapons up on deck. I ordered them to be loaded and set at the ready.

Meanwhile, the Spaniards kept firing at us. Fortunately, they were a little abaft and could only bring one of their forward guns to bear, and they missed badly every time. Our schooner went under full sail and, with a stiff morning wind, seemed to fly over the water. When the sun came up, our advantage of speed showed itself clearly, and we soon got far ahead enough for the cannon balls to fall short.

The brigantine fell further and further behind. Soon, the Spaniards—or whoever it was—must have realized the futility of their chase, for they ceased firing and then changed direction and headed out to sea, leaving us in peace. At this, sudden relief came upon us, and we broke out in loud shouts of joy.

Suddenly, Vagura, always the jester, broke into a wild, frenzied song and dance. It was really crowded on board, but this did not cramp our style, and soon, everyone—the Indians and the Africans—began to dance and leap, sing, whoop, and laugh. Only the women did not take part in the fun: they started cooking our breakfast. Neither did Arnak participate. Of all the people on board, he was the closest to my heart. He was a brave and noble man, sharp-witted and eloquent, but despite his young age—he was about twenty—he always seemed overcome with a certain sadness and reverie.

He remained standing by my side, watching the fun.

"Why don't you join in?" I asked him. "Aren't you happy at heart?"

"Yes, I am happy." He replied. "And you, Yan, why don't you dance?"

The thought that I could join the dance struck him as so humorous that a slight smile flickered on his face.

"I am not dancing because I'm steering the ship," I explained, trying to hold back a grin.

"Give it to me, then. I will take it if you would like to dance."

"You rogue! You think I am too old to dance?"

"Too old? No, no, Yan, you are not too old. You are twenty-seven, and in my village, even old men dance. But you are... too..."

"Too... what?"

"Too dignified!"

"Then take the helm! I'll show you how we dance in Virginia backwoods!"

But it did not come to that because the women called us all to eat, and the party broke up. Still, we were all very cheerful as we sat down to eat.

The brigantine had already partly disappeared over the horizon, and only her topmast still peeked out over the edge of the sea, but she was the only topic of conversation: she remained a mystery: why had the Spaniards fired on us? Some gesticulated after them with clenched fists, with curses and mockery.

Lasana brought me a bowl of hot stew of corn and gourd and set it before me with a wooden spoon.

The woman, slimmer and slightly taller than her tribesmen, with agile, graceful movements, was strikingly beautiful. People on board followed her with glances full of admiration. To my mind, she appeared like a gorgeous palm tree. Her eyes, black like coals, impossibly large, and with long eyelashes, were, despite her usual Indian reserve, so eloquent that you could read everything in them—as if her whole soul. They were lively, intelligent eyes. They showed a propensity for strong feelings and quick thinking.

She was carrying her one-year-old child strapped on her back. Hitherto depressed by Mateo's death, now—perhaps for the first time since the day of battle—she yielded to the general jubilation on board and smiled at me as she brought my meal. She didn't hide her admiration for me, watching me with undisguised pleasure: now my face, now my hands gripping the helm. Because my hands attracted so much of her attention, I asked Arnak and Vagura what she found so interesting in them. In response, she came close to me, and, placing her hands boldly on mine, she said:

A Carib Family

"Strong hands, good hands! They can be trusted!"

And I felt a warm squeeze of her small hands.

"Be careful!" I said to her. "If you embarrass me, I won't be able to steer."

"Are strong men so easy to embarrass?" she asked in mock concern. "Maybe your hands are strong, but you are weak?"

She looked playfully at her hands still lying on mine.

"I think I am weaker than you," I said.

And she—minx!—looked me in the eyes with such shameless daring that I felt a shiver in my spine.

"No, you're not weak," she said, looking me up and down.

"And how do you know that, you graceful palm?"

"I see it in your eyes. They light like the eyes of a jaguar. What did you call me?"

"A graceful palm."

"Ha! If you call me by such a beautiful name, then you are a daring hunter!" she said with an inscrutable expression on her face, in which playfulness seemed to struggle with gravity, uncertain which would win out.

"Why daring?"

"Because you are not afraid of an Indian woman!" She laughed out loud and withdrew her hands.

"You think that requires daring?" I asked.

"Oh, yes!" she laughed again.

"Noooooo..." I said. "Just a good eye and a little cunning."

At that, some funny idea came to her head: she clapped her hands with contentment.

"Tell him," she turned to Arnak and Vagura, who were translating our conversation, "tell him that a nice surprise awaits him in our village. A very nice surprise!"

"I wonder what that will be?"

"Why, we will give him the prettiest girl to wife so she may learn all about strong, good hands!"

I made an exaggerated expression of joyous expectation.

"You don't like the idea?" she asked.

"Oh, I like it! I do—as long as she is the prettiest girl. But," I pretended to worry. "Does your village have any palm trees?"

The boys screwed up their eyes. Palm trees?

"Of course, we have palm trees! Coconut palms and others," Vagura explained.

"Ah!" I sighed with exaggerated relief. "Then there will be my palm, also!"

"What palm?"

"Er... my graceful palm, of course!"

And they all exploded with laughter.

"Your promise is very generous, Graceful Palm," I continued my compliment, "because you promise me the prettiest girl in your village. But this reminds me of an old proverb my mother had taught me, my mother who had come from a distant land across the sea. Do you want to hear it?"

"Of course, we want to hear it, White Jaguar!" replied Lasana, paying me with a beautiful nickname for the one I had given her.

"The proverb says that a small bird in hand is better than a large bird high on a tree," I said.

When the boys translated the proverb for her, the woman raised her voice in feigned indignation:

"What? You call me a small bird?"

"No, no, no! It's just a proverb!" I defended myself. "You are a she-eagle!"


Thus, frolicking, we made steady and unadventurous progress east. The Spanish brigantine disappeared behind the horizon. The sea was empty and safe again.

As the sun rose and the heat became more and more unbearable, the cheerful excitement of the morning passed and turned into an ordinary day. Tormented by the heat, we all tried to find some shade to hide in, but shade was scarce on the schooner. We made a kind of awning out of a spare sail and stretched it over the main deck and a smaller one for me over the helm.

The sun was about to set when a new explosion of joy occurred among the Indians. All assembled at the prow, staring towards a distant mountain low on the horizon in the evening mist. It really had a distinctive shape, like the curved beak of a parrot pointing straight up into the sky.

I heard many mouths repeat its name.

"Mount Vulture!" Arnak translated for me.

Manauri approached me—it was again my turn to stand at the helm—and behind him came the rest: Vagura, Lasana, the Indians, the Africans. Joy was beaming on their faces. I, too, was carried away by the general excitement.

"We are approaching home," said Manauri.

How much human feeling was embedded in this simple expression, how much weight! The gloomy period of torment was coming to an end: these Indians, snatched by force from their villages, put through cruel slavery on Margarita, having rebelled, run away, and fought their way to freedom—here they were at last, looking at the unmistakable roadmark of their destination: Mount Vulture at whose feet their native villages lay.

I motioned to Arnak to take the helm and walked up to Manauri. Possessed by a sudden surge of overwhelming cordial feeling, we embraced each other like Polish people do. Joy, beaming from his face, rejuvenated him, lifted age and care from his body and visage, and the old chief suddenly looked like a youth in his twenties.


Soon, Manauri regained self-control. A strange power now lit up in his eyes, and he stared at me hard with a peculiar insistence which was at once a solemn request.

"Yan!" he began solemnly. "I come to you again with the same words I spoke a couple of days ago. Do you remember them?"

"Remind me."

"We have come to know you, Yan. We know who you are and

what you are. You are our brother, and we love you like one! We owe
our survival on the deserted island to you. Your intelligence, your
command, and your guns overcame the Spaniards. Your friendship
restored us to our former life. You are a great warrior in your country,
but you cannot return to it now because mighty enemies await you
there. Therefore, please, we ask you: stay with us. Stay forever."

And all present began to speak in a great cacophony of voices.

I took a moment to think of my reply.

Finally, I said:

"Chief Manauri! And all of you, my friends and brothers! I
thank you very much for offering me your hospitality. I feel happy and
at home with you. But I cannot accept your invitation," I declared
with great firmness. "I miss my home and my people just as you miss
yours. So, I'll only stay with you until I am ready for my departure for
the islands of the English. And when I am, can I count on your help?"

"You are our brother, Yan," replied the chief. "We will do
whatever you ask."

# The Village at the Foot
# of Mount Vulture

When we first spotted Mount Vulture, it was still many miles away.
We came into its vicinity only after many hours of sailing, and by then,
the sun was setting. There were still two full hours of sailing to the
nearest Arawak village, which lay on a lagoon at the mouth of a river
on the other side of the mountain—two hours with favorable wind
and good visibility, but the evening wind had faded, and it was growing
dark. There was no alternative but to approach the shore and drop
anchor for the night, for while the Indians knew every inch of the
seabed here, they preferred to wait until dawn and bring the schooner

into the bay in broad daylight. By the time we dropped anchor, it was completely dark, and only the light of stars lit our work. Still, nobody except the kids could think of going to sleep. The thought of the following day excited all equally: the Indians, the Africans, and me. But the Indians had expected to see some signs of life on sea or on shore, perhaps even fishermen going out to fish. But we strained our eyes in vain.

"This is strange," Manauri confided in me. "I remember well how it used to be: men always went out to fish before nightfall."

"Perhaps they were there tonight, too," I said.

"Where are they, then?"

"Perhaps they saw our ship and, fearing strangers, decided to take cover."

"I wonder," mused the chief.

On the deck, people lay in groups and talked in hushed voices, sometimes falling into contented, expectant silence. When they did, a keen ear could pick out the sounds of the land. We were no more than two or three leagues from shore, and we could hear the usual racket of the tropical night: the screaming of birds and the howling of monkeys and, a little nearer, the roar of the surf crashing on the beach. I had noticed, before it became completely dark, that the vegetation in these parts was like that I had had on Robinson Island: it was not a lush, dense forest, but high, sparse bush, dry and prickly, and within it, the familiar cacti and agaves, interspersed here and there with a few clumps of tall palms or solitary rain trees. The voices of the night emanating from the land were the same as those that had resounded in the thickets of my island, and yet, somehow, they seemed to penetrate so much deeper into the soul.

An ineffable agitation filled my heart and ignited my imagination.


And I knew why. These sounds were coming from a mighty, mysterious land covered with impenetrable forests, in whose deep, steamy shadows enormous rivers flowed, where unknown tribes of wild headhunters lurked, where cruel Spaniards and Portuguese founded white cities and imposed and enforced their law and their faith with inexorable sword and fire. These sounds came from a land that held for me an ominous, unknowable fate, endless confusion, unimaginable adventures, and inscrutable dangers. Manauri, Arnak, and Vagura sat by my side. Curious about what awaited me the next day and what kind of people I was about to meet, I began to ask the chief about the Arawak villages. I was surprised to learn that there were very few, five in all.

"Five villages? Just five?"

"Yes. Here, there are only five."

"Surely, they must be very populous?"

"Some are more populous and some less. In my village, which is the largest, there were once nearly three hundred people."

"Three hundred warriors, you mean?"

"No, no. Three hundred people in all. Men, old people, women, and children."

"So, with five villages, how many of you are there?"

"Almost a thousand."

"With women and children?"

"With women and children."

I could barely believe my ears.

"There are so few of you? Surely, you are joking!"

"No, no, I mean it."

"And that's all the Arawaks in the world?"

"Oh no! There are many more Arawaks in the world because we are a great nation. But those Arawaks do not live here but far to the south, in a country called Guyana, more than a month's march from here."

"A month's march is what—five hundred miles?"

"Maybe five hundred. Maybe more. In order to reach those Arawaks, you need to cross the Ibrinoko and then march on and on south to reach the seat of our nation."

"Ibrinoko?"

"Ibrinoko is a great river, so great you cannot see across it. The Spanish call it the Orinoco."

"So over here, there is only just this one small part of the tribe?"

"Yes. A small part."

This news disturbed me at first, for I had thought that in a large nation, there might be many sailors who could carry me to the English islands of the Caribbean Sea. But Manauri said I shouldn't worry: I'll find enough sailors. He would make sure of that.

The chief then explained to me the reasons for the odd circumstance of such a small number of Arawaks living so far away from the main body of the nation. Some five or six generations ago, he said—at least a century ago, maybe more—a sharp fratricidal strife broke out between several independent Arawak tribes in the south. No one remembers the cause of that war anymore. The villages along the Essequibo River, more populous than others, defeated and oppressed the smaller tribes. Those who lived on the banks of the Pomeroon River suffered the most, so one year, they loaded all their possessions on boats and headed north, following the seacoast, in search of a new home.

They searched for a long time because their progress was sometimes blocked by the difficult lay of the land, more often by the hostility of local tribes, but at last, they found what they'd been looking for: a good place to settle, near Mount Vulture. And they settled there. On each side, they had warlike Carib neighbors but quite distant, and after a few inconclusive skirmishes, the Caribs left them alone. Only in recent years has a new danger arisen: the Spanish slave hunters. They were now their greatest threat.

"And you, Manauri," I asked him. "Are you the chief of all the Arawaks here in the north?"

"No. Each of the five villages has its own chief, and each family lineage has its head, and I am the head of one of the lineages."

"So you people don't have a main chief, a chief over all the five villages?"

"We used to have a chief like that, Coneso. But he had very little to say, only in some very general matters."

"So, who holds all authority?"

"The village chief and the chiefs of each lineage. But their authority is limited. A chief has to listen to his people and go with what they all decide at a general meeting."

"And if, in my case, such a meeting were to decide that you should not help me return to my people because I am white?"

Manauri seemed incensed by my suggestion.

"Yan, they will not decide that. You are our friend and our savior, and such a decision could only come from people without hearts or minds. It would be disgraceful and unforgivable, a kind of madness."

"But suppose that in all the years of your absence, someone else had become chief, tasted the authority, and liked it—will he not be reluctant to accept you back in? And if he rejects you, would he not reject me, also?"

Such a thing must have been possible because Manauri suddenly fell silent. I couldn't see his face in the dark, but I guessed that it had clouded over. I guessed that he struggled with some thoughts for a moment before he replied:

"You speculate about some very remote possibilities, Yan. But no, no harm will come to you from my people, and no ingratitude. And if the tribe were to refuse you hospitality and assistance—which is unlikely but, as you say, not impossible—one thing remains certain, as certain as the existence of this sea and the existence of this mountain: we are here, we are your friends. All of us who are here on this ship are your devoted friends for life—you must accept these words. Yes, I know what I am saying: for life. Even against the will of the rest of the tribe!"

He said this with such deep conviction that my trust in him was suddenly reaffirmed. After all, we were united by the strongest ties that bind man to man: the brotherhood forged in a bloody fight for survival against a deadly enemy. Arnak and Vagura, translating the chief's words, added their own assurances of friendship, saying that they would never abandon me, ever, and having tested my young friends through thick and thin, I knew I could believe them: they would follow me to hell itself. With friends like these by my side, I could face any and all dangers in this unknown land, calling to us mysteriously over the waters.

And through the darkness of the night, there came to us howlings, cries, murmurs, crunches, croaks, sometimes so eerie and disturbing, as if they were meant to frighten and scare us. Soon, the moon emerged from the sea and lit up the landscape around the ship. The outlines of Mount Vulture lit up prominently against the starry skies, and it seemed so close as if we could but reach out and touch it. This sight greatly enlivened the Indians and reminded them of the proximity of their native village.

And since it became so bright, Manauri, Arnak, Vagura, and a few others decided to paddle ashore that night on the boats we had tied up to the schooner, visit the closest village and tell them of our arrival, then return to the ship before dawn.

"I'm going with you!" I declared.

The Indians wanted to go immediately, but Manauri delayed their departure for another hour, waiting for the moon to rise higher and the night to grow lighter.

"Do we take guns?" asked Arnak.

"No need for muskets, I think," I said. "Maybe just pistols."

"So we will prepare three pistols: for you, for me, and for Vagura."

My conversation with Manauri must have made a greater impression on the chief than I had supposed. It must have aroused concerns in him that had only smoldered in the depths of his soul until now. What reception would he get after so many years of absence? It was a troubling question.

The chief did not hide his doubts from Lasana, and while we waited for the moon to rise, he confided his hidden concerns in a quiet conversation with the young woman. It was obvious that he highly valued her opinion and prudence. They both stood on the deck close to me, almost brushing against my side, and though they muffled their voices, I involuntarily caught the drift of their words and understood the emotional charge of the conversation.

Suddenly, I thought I heard my name pronounced in Arawak. Manauri said it and then seemed to persuade Lasana about something. Unfortunately, I did not catch the drift—they were whispering, and my Arawak comprehension was really only rudimentary. Only at the end did I understand some words, insistent and pleading at the same time:

"Do this for me, Lasana. Do this for me."

And then there was silence. The woman hid in a cloak of profound silence as if weighing Manauri's words.

After a long silence, Manauri smacked his lips with impatience.

"Why do you not speak?" the chief said. And then I thought I understood: "It's so easy for you."

"You are wrong, Manauri," replied Lasana. "You are wrong. It is not easy."

Then came a torrent of words of which I understood next to nothing except the name of the old chief: Coneso. Coneso, Coneso. And another name: Pirokay.

"Pirokay, your brother?" interrupted Lasana.

"My brother." Then, more words, hushed, urgent. Something about a venomous snake. And again about me: Yan, Yan.

"Did you tell him?"

"No, no."

More words, explaining, justifying.

Then Lasana said something slowly and calmly, and I sensed resentment in her voice.

Manauri became upset and began to justify himself. But Lasana interrupted him:

"You promised him."

Manauri fell silent. Then he began pleading again. Lasana's muffled laugh rang out.

"Easy for you to say," she huffed and then fell silent.

Hearing it all, I found myself in a strange position. It never occurred to them how much I understood. Some inner devil whispered to me to play a trick on them: what if I were to turn to them and speak to them in Arawak? But I restrained myself and held my tongue. Meanwhile, Lasana, overcome with indignation, began to berate Manauri.

"What do you imagine?" Mateo. Yan. Mateo. "No, no, no!"

And then, in a flash, I understood everything: Manauri, worried about the reception he might receive in the village, wanted to bind me to himself and his group as tightly as possible and was trying to persuade Lasana to take me on as a lover in order to achieve that end.

"Say, do you hate him?"

"No," she replied simply.

"You see?"

"No, I don't see. You don't see!"


Crossing the calm sea did not present any difficulties. There were eleven of us. Two boats accommodated us all.

We jumped ashore one after the other, each one sensing the extraordinary weight of the moment: we were each stepping into a new chapter of his life. After blowing me all the way here from my distant Virginia, where would my fate take me next?

We set out at once, walking single file. The Indians glided noiselessly like cats. I alone walked heavily and noisily; in view of the numerous poisonous snakes in these parts, especially active at night, Manauri had advised me to put on a pair of Spanish boots once we reached the shore.

"Why only me?" I objected.

"You are not from here. You do not sense snakes in the dark."

"And you do?"

"Oh, yes! Vipers—we do."

It was a nice pair of boots, so I put them on obediently, and now, as we marched, I thumped the ground mercilessly, and my footsteps echoed for a quarter of a mile.

But we weren't worried about making a racket: we were in our own country, near our friends. Our path took us around the base of Mount Vulture, first along the coast, then turned right into the bush. After a while, we reached the bay. It wasn't really a bay but a lagoon half a mile wide, with a fairly wide opening to the sea. Manauri pointed to the opposite shore of the lagoon and said calmly:

"Our village is over there."

At the edge of the water on the opposite side, we could make out some structures, perhaps huts, but it was difficult to see clearly despite the moonlight.

"Are there dogs in the village?" I asked.

"Of course!"

"Many?"

"Oh, yes!"

"So why don't we hear them?"

The strange silence confused Manauri and the rest of the Indians, too. Could the dogs be sleeping? That was impossible. In every village in the Virginia forest, there was always some dog barking at night somewhere, so why not here? And the sound should carry well over the water. While the alarmed Indians were expressing various speculations, we continued our journey along the shore of the lake. The terrain was the same as before: sand, covered in places with thickets, here and there with rocks. Here and there, the rocks came all the way down to the water, creating some strange caves and pools by the lake. By now, we had reached halfway around the lagoon and could distinguish individual huts scattered in the river valley.

And there was still no sign of life. The deathly silence seemed so unnatural to me that I stopped our march.

"No sign of dogs!" I said.

"There are no dogs," Manauri did not hide his concern.

"But the huts are there, the village is there," observed Arnak.

"Yes, the huts stand where they were. But something is amiss."

"There are no people," I declared. "Something's seriously wrong. Let's be extra careful. This could be a trap."

I regretted that we had not brought our guns—why, we even had no bows with us! But it was too late to remedy that. We now had to find an explanation for the mystery. Vagura approached me and asked in a whisper choked with excitement:

"Do you think something had happened here? Some misfortune?"

"Something had to have happened, that's for sure! There are no people!"

"Maybe the Spaniards came and took everyone?"

"We will know soon enough when we get there."

Snakes or no snakes, we had to move quietly, so I took off my damned boots and sighed a great sigh of relief: walking barefoot for over a year had somehow changed the shape of my feet, and the blasted boots pinched me like the devil. How pleasant it was to put my unencumbered feet on the cool sand! I stuffed my boots in the hollow of a tree growing on the shore of the lagoon and was glad to be rid of the curse. We now walked extra quietly and snuck from bush to bush, and soon, we got to the first hut. Its walls were made of pleated reed, its roof of coconut fronds. One glance was enough to see that the cottage had been uninhabited for a long time and was on the verge of collapsing. The reed walls leaned in all directions, and the moon shone through a great hole in the roof.

"Go, look inside," Manauri ordered Arnak. Hidden in the shadow of the thicket, we waited for the boy's return.

"Do you remember who lived here?" I asked Manauri.

"I remember. Mabukuli, my friend."

"And when the Spaniards attacked you, he was not captured?"

"No. He was not here on the night of the attack."

"So, following the attack, he could have returned here and

continued to live here?”

“Yes.”

Arnak returned from the hut and reported that he found nothing suspicious: some items of lesser importance, such as gourds for the carrying of water, were still there, and the hut made the impression of having been abandoned by the inhabitants.

“No signs of violence?” asked the chief.

“No.”

Silence reigned all around. Everything pointed to one conclusion: the village had been deserted.

My Indian friends were stunned by the emptiness of the place and soon became overcome by a great sadness, which affected me, too.

The abandoned village presented us with an ominous mystery. As we approached the hut, I warned my comrades not to go in unnecessarily: we could not be sure whether some plague had not driven the residents away.

Moving on, we passed the ruins of another hut. And now one of the Indians recalled seeing it burn during the Spanish attack. This meant that the hut had burnt, then was rebuilt, and only then abandoned. The residents left the village sometime *after* the Spanish attack. We discovered various traces suggesting the village was abandoned long ago: at least a year ago, perhaps two.

In a somber and depressed mood, we walked carefully to the end of the village, finding all the huts empty and abandoned. They did not stand all together but were scattered at some distance from each other over perhaps ten acres of land.

Finally, our path was blocked by the river emptying into the lagoon. At the bank, we sat down on the ground under a large tree to hold council together.

“One thing is certain,” I announced in a half-whisper. “There was no fighting here.”

A general murmur of agreement answered me.

“There are no signs of fighting anywhere, not an arrowhead, not even a broken spear. Nothing,” Manauri confirmed.

"But where could they have gone?" wondered Arnak.

"Perhaps inland, further from the coast," I ventured a guess. "Perhaps for safety from the Spanish. There may have been more slave-catcher attacks."

These words seemed as if I had taken them out of the mouths and hearts of my comrades. We all seized on this interpretation because it offered us hope that the tribe was still alive, that it had not succumbed to disease or been carried off into slavery.

"Perhaps, yes, perhaps they moved further from the sea," Manauri supposed. "If so, we will find them easily tomorrow."

"And the other villages, the other four, where are they?" I asked.

"Along this river, upstream."

"Far from here?"

"No, not far. The closest village is maybe an hour by boat."

An hour by boat.

"Close," I said.

The chief, seeing my face, immediately guessed my train of thought.

"I know what you think!" he said. "We must go there and see how things stand there."

"Of course! Perhaps these people joined that village."

We checked the moon and the stars—we still had half the night ahead of us. We had to get back to the schooner before dawn, but it was advisable to ascertain the situation as much as possible beforehand so that we would have something to report and some basis to form a plan of action. Manauri selected four Indians familiar with the area and sent them upriver, telling them to be quick. We were going to wait for their return near the lagoon.

The ground near the river was wet, swampy, and covered with dense, lush vegetation. An overpowering stench of moldy leaves and rotting roots hung thickly in the air, almost dulling the senses. The belt of vegetation by the riverside was narrow, no wider than thirty or forty paces, but out of that thicket now came fantastic noises as if whole tribes of ravenous beasts were devouring each other within. There was rattling, screaming, screeching, moaning, knocking, and, worst of all, bone-chilling hissing. You would say: the gates of hell had opened there, releasing all kinds of monsters to our damnation.

The nights in the Virginian forest had their voices, too; as did the bush on the deserted island, which we had left recently, but I had never heard such uproar as this in my life.

My Indians, used to such noises, paid them no attention.

"These ear-piercing hisses," I asked. "Are they insects?"

"Yes. Insects," replied Manauri.

A creature meowed menacingly.

"And was that a cat? A wild cat?" I shuddered at the memory of the jaguar.

"No. It's a tree frog."

Then, there was a loud metallic knocking as if a man were sharpening a scythe.

"And this? Is this a bird?"

"No, that too was a frog, but in the river."

Suddenly, there was a dull squawk and a splash in the water. Manauri listened carefully for a while.

"That—I don't know what that is," he admitted. "Maybe a large water rat."

"Are you sure it was not a large predator? Don't you have them here?"

"Maybe it was. We do have them here."

The chief looked about calmly and impassively and said:

"Probably not in this narrow stretch, though."

There was another characteristic feature of this place, a particularly unpleasant one: the plague of mosquitoes. Thousands, millions of mosquitoes. Whole clouds surrounded us and stung like the devil. The Indians seemed accustomed to it and bravely endured the plague, patiently swatting themselves. But I was close to madness. Finally, I took myself away from the riverside and up a sandy hill, where there was a little breeze and a spot of respite from the little monsters. Satisfied, I sat on the sand and waited.

Clouds began to swirl and roll across the sky, covering the moon. Then, almost complete darkness enveloped us. Although Manauri reassured me that there were probably no large predators here, yet there was enough of a hunter in me not to forget even for a moment that this forest was home to all sorts of dangerous man-eaters. So, I took the precaution of checking the gunpowder in my pistol.

And I did right, for as I sat there staring at the darkness around me, it seemed to me that I sensed a suspicious movement in the nearby bush.

A delusion of the senses? But no. No! My heart gave a violent start—Boom! Boom! Boom! There was no doubt: a large shadow glided between two agave plants. I drew the pistol from my belt as quietly as I could and aimed it at the animal. Immediately, the thought arose in me whether it was a good idea to alarm the whole neighborhood by firing a shot while the situation was still uncertain. Behold, I gathered from the movements of the creature that it did not guess my presence, its attention turned entirely in the direction of the river where my companions sat. The creature was quite tall, I thought, though the darkness made it difficult to make out its shape. I assumed it was a great ape rather than a quadruped. To shoot or not to shoot? I was still hesitating. The distance was only a few paces. Just in case, I cocked my pistol as quietly as I could. But I failed: the cock clicked, there was a sudden crash in the bush, and the animal was gone. I decided I had had enough of my romantic solitude.

Going back down to the river, to my Indians, I thought of this rich, fascinating, and dangerous land where my fate had thrown me. This was not my idyllic Robinson Island, where, after killing the great serpent and slaying the stray jaguar, I lived among harmless animals, on the lookout at most against a few vipers. Here was another world! Here, the forest seethed with an inexhaustible profusion of wild creatures; here, the beasts were large, audacious, and aggressive. I told my companions about the animal I had spotted on the hill and about my guess that it was a monkey.

"A monkey?" Manauri was surprised. "Impossible."

"So what could it have been?"

"Some other beast. Maybe a tapir?"

"How tall is a tapir?"

"It's pretty tall. And heavy."

But the animal seemed rather agile to me, not heavy.

"Maybe a puma? Was it fawn?"

"It was rather dark."

"Hm... we don't have big monkeys here, and they all stay in the trees anyway. They rarely come down to the ground."

Our scouts soon returned, and the bad news they brought from upriver devastated us: most likely, all four Arawak villages had been abandoned. The village upriver was empty, and all the huts had mostly collapsed, overgrown with weed and vine.

"Then there is no point bringing the ship into the lagoon," someone observed.

"And do what instead?" I asked.

"Sail on east, then south, down to the river Pomeroon. There, we will meet our kinsmen, the other Arawaks."

"I don't recommend that!" I objected. "Remember yesterday's ship, how it chased us? When the Spanish realize that we wiped out their search party on Robinson Island and stole their schooner, they will start looking for us all over and will soon spot us at sea!"

"So what do you advise?"

"I would bring the ship into the lagoon, hide it so that it is not visible from the sea, and stay in hiding for a couple of weeks. And then, take the ship out and sail like mad for your Pomeroon."

"Yan advises well!" Arnak supported me. "To wander on the high seas now would only get us in trouble. Better we hide here."

"Yes, that's what I think too!" Manauri agreed. "And I think we should look again at these villages during daytime because we may have missed something. Perhaps we'll find some explanation as to why our people left."

We got up and started for the shore immediately. The two

men whom we intended to leave behind in the old village to await our arrival walked us as far back as the tree where I had left my boots.

"Will you wear them?" asked Vagura.

"He will!" replied Manauri, deeply concerned, as you can see, for my precious life.

"Very well, have it your way," I grumbled with resignation.

Vagura ran up to the tree. After a moment, we heard his muffled exclamation of surprise. We approached.

"Your boots! They're gone!" he announced, quite confused.

The tree was the same, and the hollow was there, but the boots were gone.

"What happened here?" exclaimed Manauri. "Witchcraft?"

"I was there when Yan hid the boots! I saw it! It was this tree, this hollow!" Vagura assured us. "Someone stole them!"

"Someone has been spying on us," said Arnak in a hushed voice and looked around carefully.

Suddenly, one of the Indians, seized with terror, began to whisper madly that he knew the culprit: it was the terrible *kanaima* who had cast a spell on the villages to make them empty and now stolen my boots.

"The *kanaima* killed everybody and now is going to kill us!"

"Oh, shut your stupid mouth," interrupted him Manauri choking with anger. "Stop raving like an old woman!"

"He's not raving!" another Indian came to the defense of the scolded man. "Can't you see, chief, what has happened in these villages? Something terrible must have happened! There are no inhabitants! Someone exterminated them! Who? And now those boots!"

"*Kanaima*! It had to be *kanaima*!" several others whispered with trembling lips.

"Let's get out of here! This is an enchanted place! Evil ghosts will kill us! *Kanaima*!"

I turned hastily to Arnak:

"Who is this *kanaima*?"

"A spirit of revenge! Whenever something bad happens, people think it is *kanaima*."

Some of the Indians, moved by superstitious fear, actually wanted to flee. The most affected—literally, on the verge of losing his mind—was the fellow who had first pronounced the word *kanaima*. He was visibly trembling.

This whole thing seemed completely incomprehensible to me because I knew the man as a fearless warrior: only four days ago, he stood up against the Spanish in the thick of the bloodiest battle. I now had an inkling of the terrible fetters of superstition and ignorance that suffocated the souls of these people.

With great difficulty, Manauri managed to control the situation. While he reasoned with his men, I remembered the moment when, on the sandy hill, I saw that shadow of a mysterious animal. I now realized that it had not been a beast; it had been a man! Of course, it had been a man sneaking in the bush!

"Fellows!" I whispered with emphasis. "Now I understand!"

When I announced my guess to my companions, they came around to my interpretation. We all understood in an instant who had taken my boots. Suddenly, the fear of ghosts dissipated, and the *kanaima* ceased to frighten. But in its stead, a far more dangerous threat appeared before us. Who was the man? Or these men? Were they friend or foe?

Despite this worry, we did not give up our plan to hide the schooner in the lagoon and wait out a few weeks in the area. Right now, the greatest danger lay at sea.

We resumed our march towards the sea. Nobody accosted us. A few hundred paces from the tree with the hollow, in a thick bush, Vagura and his two companions quietly separated from us and dove into shadows. They were going to stay behind and keep their ears and eyes open, watching over the area during our absence. We left them all our pistols.

taken them, I would have heard of that.”

“And how did it happen that you were left alone, Arasibo?”

The Indian winced, which made him look even uglier. I felt sorry for the fellow because he probably wasn’t as evil as he looked.

“Before we left, I went hunting on the river,” he said grimly. “A huge cayman attacked me and ripped my leg up. I had quite a fight with him, but eventually, I chased him off. But I lost so much blood that I passed out and lay on the shore senseless, no one knows how long. It’s a good thing the beast didn’t come back for me, or he could have eaten me then. How many days I lay like this, I don’t know. My fellows found me on the eve of their departure. The boats had already gone out to sea. With my leg, like it was, I could not go with them. Besides, the old sorcerer, Carapana, hated me because...”

He paused, uncertain whether to finish his thought.

“Because of what?” Manauri pressed him.

Arasibo waved his hands and winced to indicate that the story wasn’t worth telling.

“Oh, speak, you ugly cockroach, speak up!” the chief insisted. “We’re not his friends either. Tell us!”

“Carapana hated me because I had figured out his spells. He was afraid I would take his power away from him. He turned Coneso against me. So Coneso did not let the others carry me, and he ordered me left behind. By doing it, he condemned me to death. Everyone else went south, and I was left here to starve. The family left me some food, but they had to go. And yet, I survived! I have healed, and I have lived! And, as you see, I can walk again!”

And he started laughing an evil, bitter laugh. A scathing grimace flitted across his face: the part about him being able to walk was clearly a gallows joke.

“Coneso is still chief? ” growled Manauri angrily. “And Carapana is still with him?”

“Yes, he is still chief. And Carapana is with him.”

And thus, our position became clear to us.

Clear? Never has this word sounded with such cruel irony as it did in this case! It became suddenly as clear as daylight that we were all alone and could not count on any help; that our Arawak tribe had wandered off into the unknown—and good luck finding them! And thus, my plans for an imminent departure for the English Antilles had just taken a huge setback. I could do nothing without the help of my comrades, and they, eager to return to their own people after so many years of captivity, would now never be persuaded to embark on a new and dangerous voyage over the sinister Caribbean Sea instead. I said nothing of this to Manauri, knowing full well what his reply would be: "Come with us to our villages on the Pomeroon and be our guest there. You will not lack a thing, and then we will then see how we can help you!"

Besides, I realized that my Indians had also found themselves in a difficult position. The area was clearly dangerous, and the Spaniards far too close for them to remain here for any length of time. Arasibo painted the ruthlessness and cruelty of the people of *La Soledad* in very stark colors: that their numbers were great, that they wanted to enslave everyone under their ruthless paws, that they constantly patrolled the area, and that many Cumanágoto were in their service.

"Who are Cumanágoto?"

"Cumanágoto are a neighboring tribe to the west of here," explained Manauri. "They are an aggressive, ruthless lot. And they hunt men."

"What? Hunt men? Are they cannibals?"

"Oh, yes!" said the chief. "We had a lot of trouble with them. They are real Caribs."

"And Caribs are dangerous?"

"O, yes! They are evil, warlike, wild. There are many tribes of Caribs, but all of them like war better than planting corn."

"And you people are not Caribs?"

Manauri, Arasibo, and all the others were shocked that anyone could possibly mistake them for Caribs.

"No!" exclaimed Manauri. "I see you don't understand! We,

128

the Arawaks, are a different tribe. We are a decent, peace-loving people. We live off the land and forest, not off war."

"Oh, I know this about you!" I tried to appease them.

Turning now to the topic of the *La Soledad* Spaniards, I wondered whether Arasibo was not exaggerating their strength but soon decided that even if his story contained only a small grain of truth, it was disturbing enough.

The women called us to breakfast, our first meal on the mainland, to which Arasibo—a sworn enemy of all crocodiles for life—contributed some cayman meat. I must admit that it tasted delicious, a little reminiscent of veal, but smelled a bit of mud.

Immediately after breakfast, everyone, including the women, sat down in the shade of one of the huts for a general council. On the most important point, all were of the same mind: that we should leave the area as soon as possible and go south in search of the Arawaks. But different opinions soon emerged regarding the question of how to proceed: by land or by sea. I now spoke in favor of taking the sea: I felt sorry to abandon such a beautiful ship to the Spanish. Besides, as long as I held onto it, I retained the option of using it for my voyage to the English isles one day in the future. But my companions were of another opinion. They were afraid of the sea. The encounter with the Spanish brigantine the day before had left an indelible mark on them and persuaded them to stay on land. They insisted on marching overland.

"Don't worry, Yan!" Manauri assured me. "With or without the schooner, we will get you to your island. You will see."

"I believe you, and I trust you," I replied. "But we have so many possessions on board, we cannot carry everything on our backs. Just think, we have thirty guns, a dozen and a half pistols, whole barrels of powder, and sacks of lead! What shall we do with it? How can we give up so much precious treasure? Besides, we need to take a lot of food with us, too!"

What Arasibo had said about the *La Soledad* ranch and Manauri about the Cumanágoto gave me a bad feeling about crossing the land on foot. Men were preying on each other here, and guns could well prove critical, not only for our own survival but also for the survival of the whole tribe in the future. It seemed a pity to abandon them. But how were we to carry them overland when we would have a lot of other necessary baggage besides provisions? But Manauri offered sound advice:

"We will take with us as much as we can carry. The rest we will bury underground. Later, we will return here with more men and recover it all."

"And the schooner?"

"I suspect that neither you nor we will ever have any use for it. But, just in case, we will hide it. We can drag it a few hundred paces upriver and moor it there, where the trees will hide it from the shore. And if you really need the ship later, we will come back to get it."

"Yes, Yan!" They all began to try to convince me. "We will not abandon or waste anything!"

The chief's plan was solid. We resolved that we would leave the following day since that day, we had a lot of work to do: unload the ship, bury excess gear in a safe place, then hide the schooner upriver. At the end of the meeting, I noticed some commotion among the people. They whispered something amongst themselves and kept glancing in the direction of other huts.

There, I saw Arasibo walking towards us, holding a pair of Spanish boots in front of him, the cause of our fears the night before. The Indian limped slowly, with the solemn air of a priest bearing a sacred relic. With that impassive face, he reached us and approached me amid the general silence. All stared at us, captivated as if they were watching a bizarre religious ceremony. Vagura—always the joker— broke the silence with a snort of suppressed laughter.

"Your boots have found you!" he said to me. "There is no escaping them now!"

Arasibo stood before me and placed the boots solemnly at my feet. And they were serious boots: massive, huge, hard as a tool of torture, with uppers reaching above the knee. And if you wore them, when we enter our village, you will wear the Spanish captain's uniform and the boots."

"We are going to take that uniform with us, too?" I panicked.

"Yes, we will."

"Very well, if you insist, I will deck myself out on our arrival. But just for our entry. Then, I will take it all off."

"That is fine. But you will also put it on whenever other chiefs visit our village, OK?"

I looked at Manauri with admiration. The man deserved to be a tribal chief: he clearly understood the political importance of pomp and circumstance.

The Spanish boots were too big for Arasibo, but he didn't care. He assured us that they made it easier for him to walk.

We now began to debate what to do with the man and whether or not to bring him with us. For his part, he assured us that his lameness did not prevent him from marching briskly and begged that we do not leave him behind. Some shook their heads at this, fearing he might cause trouble on the march and cause unnecessary delays. They urged him to stay at Mount Vulture for the time being and go south only with the warriors who would return here to collect the rest of our possessions.

When Arasibo heard this, wild despair shrunk his face, and his pupils ignited with mad, hateful fire.

"You do me wrong!" he wheezed, unable to speak coherently. "Wrong! Wrong! Wrong!"

He became so agitated that I felt that I needed to step in and speak up for him.

"Manauri!" I called out loud in order to cut through the din of all the voices. "Is it *necessary* that Arasibo stay here to guard our possessions?"

"It would be good," replied the chief. "Yes."

"But is it *necessary*?"

"Necessary?" he hesitated under my sharp glance. "Necessary? No, I guess it is not necessary. No."

"So it does not matter if he stays or not?"

"No, I guess it does not matter."

"And you, Arasibo! Are you sure that you are strong enough to handle the hardships of the march?"

"Strong enough, yes! I promise I will not delay your march!" whimpered the lame man. "My leg has healed. Yes, it is a little shorter, but the boots will help!"

"All right!" I ruled. "Then we will take him with us! It would be too cruel to leave him behind."

The group did not object, for, in fact, they all felt sorry for him. Arasibo scowled at me and pursed his lips in an odd expression of thanks: he was one strange, grumpy creature.

We immediately set about the most urgent work on the ship. The Indians, most of whom knew every bend in the river, pulled the ship into a place where the river spilled wide and deep, and we anchored the schooner there and tied it to the trees. There was a cavern nearby at the foot of a rock, only a few dozen paces from the water, and into it, we carried all the things we could not take with us. There were quite a lot of them because not only were we leaving behind a part of our guns, well protected with grease, but also a lot of various tools, provisions of corn and dried meat which we had found on the schooner, and all the rigging of the ship. We finished all the work by the afternoon, then covered the entry to the cave with stones and brushwood so that no stranger would suspect anything. We took three of our boats ashore and hid them in the bushes, placing them upside down.

# Damned Spaniards Again

The next day at sunrise, after a night's sleep on the shore of the lagoon, we set off on our way. Each of us carried a large bundle on his back,

# Arasibo

At dawn, we raised anchor and set off with the morning breeze. The mouth of the bay, or whatever you called it—the mouth of the lagoon—was some two hundred paces wide. The passage was shallow, so Manauri and his Indians stared hard into the water to find our way among the shallows. Fortunately, the schooner did not have a deep draft and passed smoothly over all obstacles, and when the first rays of the sun blushed the mountainside, we were already entering the quiet waters of the bay.

"No brigantine will ever enter this bay," observed Arnak.

"You are right. We should be safe from the sea in here."

Far away, on the southwest horizon of the lagoon, we saw the ruined huts of the abandoned village. We studied the whole shoreline but did not detect a living soul other than four figures standing at the edge of the water and waving to us with their hands.

"Over there! Our Vagura! I recognize him!" exclaimed Manauri, full of surprise.

"But there are four of them!" I said. "One too many."

Through the spyglass, I saw our three companions and a fourth, a stranger, in their midst. He was an Indian. Our men seemed to treat him in a friendly manner. I handed the spyglass to Manauri.

"Ah!" he sighed with great emotion the instant he glanced through the glass.

"Do you recognize him?"

"Yes. He's from my lineage. Arasibo."

"So there has remained a trace of your former life here!"

"Apparently, yes!"

We approached the place where the four Indians were waiting for us. The bay was fairly deep here. We sounded it at six fathoms. We dropped anchor no more than sixty paces from the beach.

The joy of the unexpected meeting was very great, but the Indians did not show it too much, either with gestures or with words;

only their eyes shone with emotion: such was their custom at solemn moments. Arasibo, a stocky, short man in his prime, had a severe limp in one leg. There was a kind of cunning intent in his pupils, but not wanting to misjudge him, I assumed his handicap gave him a frustrated appearance. He was damn ugly, though, and his ugliness was compounded by the malicious expression of little, penetrating eyes set way too close together in a kind of permanent squint.

His story partly confirmed our nocturnal guesses. The Arawaks had left their settlements without a fight, albeit not entirely voluntarily. They did this in fear of another attack by the Spaniards because now the slavers did not only come from the sea. Two years ago, a large Spanish ranch named *La Soledad* had been set up some twenty miles to the west of the lagoon in an area of undulating steppe. The settlers had brought large herds of cattle from the city of Cumaná and claimed the whole surrounding country together with all the Indians inhabiting it and announced that they would ruthlessly exterminate any recalcitrants who opposed the new government. And theirs had not been empty words. The Arawaks were the first obliged to bend their neck under the yoke of the conquistadors. Too few and too ill-armed to fight, they had only one way to escape forced labor on the ranch: to flee. And that's what they did: they left two years ago.

"And did they manage to get away?"

"Yes! They ran away south, towards the old Arawak country in Guyana. Mostly, they went on foot through the steppe, towards the Orinoco River, and then crossed it to reach their old home on the shores of the Pomeroon River. Others loaded their possessions onto boats. They rowed along the shore of the sea, and, though in a roundabout way, they also reached the Pomeroon."

"And how do you know that they have reached their destination?"

Arasibo frowned, thinking.

"Well, those on the boats must have kept close to the shore, so they could not have drowned or gone astray, yes? As for the others—those who walked across the steppe—if the *Soledad* Spaniards had they were as hot as hell.

"It's the *kanaima*!" I jokingly shouted, pointing to my boots as if tormented, evoking the name of the vengeful spirit.

Arnak and Lasana laughed, but Manauri preserved a serious expression. Some frowned at hearing me invoke the name of the demon.

"Yan! We do not want you to get bitten by a snake," said the chief. "You are a precious brother to us, and there are plenty of snakes here. Listen up, people! Are there vipers here, yes or no?" he asked the rest of the Indians.

"There are! There are! Plenty! Big ones, too!" all earnestly confirmed.

"We honor our chiefs with feathered caps decorating their heads," Manauri continued relentlessly. "Whereas you... we will honor you with these boots decorating your feet!"

"They pinch like the devil!" I objected. "They bake my feet! You can't make me wear them!" I defended myself as best I could.

"Life brings many heavy burdens which we must bear patiently," Manauri said in an admonishing voice. "In these boots, you will look distinguished, respectable, powerful, and invincible."

"But I will be sore and unhappy," I waved my hands in opposition. "Come on, wise chief, in the name of god, do not make me do this."

But Manauri was not inclined to be merciful, stubbornly insisted, and did not intend to budge. He spoke to me in polite words but with an unwavering expression and a hard look in his eyes:

"I ask you, Yan, don your beautiful boots! They will be a mark of your dignity!"

The good Manauri had apparently devised for me some role of a ceremonial chief and chosen these nasty boots as my insignia of power. The devil take him! What was worse, other Indians seemed to share his view and got it into their heads that it was my honorable duty to wear these boots. Have they all lost their minds?

Only Arnak and Lasana did not take part in the general

argument. They kept calm and were clearly having great fun at my expense. They had no intention of coming to my rescue. As for Vagura, his eyes sparkled with hilarity. He chuckled, addressing me in English:

"Your boots have caught you! You will now be a Jaguar in Boots!"

He remembered—the cruel scoffer—that Lasana had called me White Jaguar, and he was determined to milk that for all the fun he could get.

Of the whole group, only Arasibo was an exception. He was still standing next to the boots and, immobile, was watching me intently. He watched my eyes and lips and was thinking something, calculating. The intensity of internal effort twisted his ugly face in a terrible grimace.

What did Arasibo want from me? How much intense desire was in that ugly face, in those little penetrating eyes!

Suddenly, I understood.

With a cunning smile, I turned to the chief:

"Well, then, Manauri, you say these are my boots?"

"They are! They are!"

"Very well then!"

I lifted them from the ground, and I handed them to Arasibo.

"There! I gift them to you!"

The chief seemed to puff up with indignation, but Arnak, Vagura, and Lasana exploded with such wholehearted and catching laughter, and Arasibo put my boots on with such lighting speed and dexterity that there was nothing left for him to do. He laughed with the rest of us and waved his hand, admitting his defeat.

When the laughter died down, Manauri declared:

"Very well, Yan. This time, I give in. But you have to promise us two things, and both are for your own good."

"As it is a request between brothers, I agree in advance."

"First: always, always, always watch your step, watch the ground and beware of snakes. And second, and equally important,

A Boa Constrictor

even though we took only the most necessary items. In addition to the Indian weapons—bows, javelins, and clubs—we had three muskets, three fowling pieces, five pistols, a decent supply of powder and shot, a dozen axes, knives, shovels, and many provisions for at least at the beginning of our march we wanted to waste as little time as possible hunting and foraging, and finally some fabrics and Spanish clothes, among which reigned supreme the captain's parade uniform, intended for me to wear on great ceremonial occasions.

Our path led along the bank of the river, which emptied into the lagoon. In the morning, we passed the abandoned Arawak villages, all presenting the same sad picture of utter abandonment. About noon, we rested, and then, leaving the valley of the river, we crossed a chain of rather steep and difficult hills that ran parallel to the seashore. In the evening, we went over a high pass and began a descent into the valley on the other side. The land here was easier, with gentler ravines and more convenient for walking. We camped on its edge, totally exhausted.

All day, Arasibo had bravely kept up with us. We encountered little vegetation, for the area had a dry climate, and there were few trees, mostly bushes, but prickly like the devil and scratching the skin mercilessly. Of game, we saw not a trace. I searched in vain for parrots, my dear friends from Robinson Island, but there were no birds at all other than vultures which circled overhead, making me wonder what prey those scavengers were hoping to find in this barren land if not us, humans. Among the black monsters, there once appeared a rare vulture, very beautifully colored. He had a white neck and a red head. The Indians closely followed its flight, welcoming it with joy, for it was a bird-hero of their myths, Arnak explained to me: the forefather of all other vultures.

The dawn of the next day found us already on the march.

After we left the mountain range and descended through the foothills to the plain below, a wide, lush steppe surrounded us. Slightly undulating, overgrown with tall grasses, with bushes hidden in ravines and hollows here and there, and a few sparse, solitary trees. They were palm trees with peculiar leaves which I had never seen before. Their fronds did not have the elongated shape like the coconut palms, similar to girls' braids, nor were they feathery like other palms I had seen, but somewhat disconcertingly, they resembled enormous spread-out human hands. Menacing as they looked, they diverted the eye amid the monotony of the steppe. They grew sparsely, several hundred paces apart or more. They did not form a dense grove anywhere and did not obstruct the view, so we had a clear line of sight for miles but also no shade to hide in.

"What a superb, rich, delightful sea of grass! And it is endless, endless!" I called out at one point, overcome with wonder, as we stood on some small hillock gazing around us in all directions.

"The Spanish call this *llanos*," Manauri said. "Are you eager to see its end? Oh, we are far, very far from its end! Going straight south, it takes ten days to reach the Orinoco River, and all this time, you walk through this grass. But things would be very different if we turned east instead!"

"How different is the East?"

"There, in just two or three days, the grass stops, and the forest begins. The same forest which covers the mouth of the Orinoco and grows along the sea. It covers the entire country to the east. It is a huge, vast, thick, dense forest. It is said that a man's life is not long enough to cross it. And there are many rivers that run through it, and many, many Indians live within it. All sorts of tribes are there, both benign and warlike, some more similar to wild beasts than men, some prosperous and some wretched. And there is also a tribe who is said to have more gold than we have corn and to build its huts of gold!"

"Oh, you probably mean the gold of the Incas!" I interrupted him. "But the Spaniards have conquered that nation a long time ago!"

"In which case, these people are not the Incas you say. This tribe remains unconquered and is called the Manao.[3] And they live in

---

[3] The Manao, now extinct branch of the Arawak family, have given their name to the city of Manaus in the heart of the Amazon jungle.

villages built of gold."

"This sounds like a fairy tale to me."

"Maybe it is a fairy tale, but who knows? In our tribe, among the Arawaks, there is a story from ancient times about many Spanish expeditions who went up the Caroni River[4] to conquer the Manao and take their gold. And they found it but failed to win the war, and few ever returned."

"And does this gold-bearing Caroni really exist?"

"Oh, yes, Yan, it does! It enters the Orinoco from the south. It is a great river flowing through a dense jungle, but it does not create many channels or many islands like the Orinoco... Instead, it flows quick and straight and descends in many steep waterfalls. That forest in the south is a terrible forest, mysterious and dangerous."

"And your river, the Pomeroon, also flows through that forest?"

"Oh, yes! But it does not enter the Orinoco. It has its own outlet to the sea. It is ten or twelve days' march south from the Orinoco. The Arawaks have cleared some fields there, where they live and grow maize, but all around them is the same endless forest!"

Thus, chatting about faraway places, great rivers, and the mysterious forest, whose tropical splendor, unfamiliar to me and difficult to comprehend, enticed me greatly—we plunged into the tall grass of the *llanos*.

The summer rains had just ended, so the grass grew lush and, in places, reached above our heads, but most often, it reached to our waist and, in patches, only to the knees.

We followed the Indian custom of walking single file, and whoever led the way made a path for the others, either with his own body or by slashing in front of him with a long knife. It was warm and pleasant at sunrise, but within two hours, the heat became unbearable, and we roasted in the cruel sun. The hitherto azure sky turned livid, a leaden hue, and dense, hot air rolled over the steppe like water.

---

[4] A right bank tributary of the Orinoco.

Suddenly, Manauri, walking in front, stopped our procession and, ordering everyone to be quiet, beckoned me to him with a wave of his hand.

"Look!" he pointed to the ground when I approached.

There were fresh tracks of animals that had recently passed this way. Judging from the broad swathes of flattened grass, it was a large herd of substantial beasts.

"Wild buffalo?" I asked Manari.

But neither Manauri nor anyone else knew what a buffalo was, and when I described the animals to them, they said that there were no such animals here.

"So what are these beasts? What is the mystery?"

The Indians, proficient nature experts, in vain searched their minds for an answer.

The animal trail approached our path at an angle and proceeded further, more or less in the same direction as we did. We took advantage of the path they had cleared and followed in the footsteps of animals.

We did not go more than a hundred steps when I saw animal dung on the ground and at once understood everything: it was cattle. Cattle had passed this way, and judging from the freshness of the excrement, it was close. Indeed, soon, we saw them: a herd of several dozen animals slowly marching across the *llanos*.

"Fresh meat!" the chief's eyes lit up with delight.

"Where there are cattle, there will be Spaniards!" I warned him. But I did not insist on the warning too much because, like everyone else, I began to drool at the mouth.

We decided to kill one or two animals, but it seemed safer to us to leave the animal trail line and approach the animals from another side. We looked around to see if the area was safe and whether there were no men around.

"Yan! What is this?" exclaimed Arnak suddenly, pointing towards the back, in the direction from which we had come.

In the distance, about two miles behind us, we saw something indistinct, a peculiar dark point. It was moving. Another herd of cattle? I put the spyglass to my eye and immediately understood: they were riders, men on horseback, galloping in our direction. I shouted to my companions. The riders were not following our footsteps but the tracks of the cattle, but there was little consolation in that, for they would be upon us in a few minutes. There was only one chance to avoid meeting them.

"Quick! Into the grass!" I yelled. "Run single file so that they don't know how many of us there are!"

There was no need to repeat myself: everyone understood what had to be done. The head of the procession turned to the left of the animal trail. Arnak, Vagura, Manauri, and Miguel ran up to me while others followed the leader into the grass.

"How many?" boomed the chief.

"A few. Six, seven."

"Spaniards?"

"Yes... Arnak, Vagura! Are your guns loaded?"

"Yes, they are!"

"Check your powder! Who's got the pistols?"

"I do!" exclaimed Miguel and dropped his bag to take them out.

Soon, we had the firearms in our hands. We wasted no time loading them. The *llanos* were flat like a table here, without any prominences or depressions, and as if to spite us, the grass wasn't very high, either: it barely reached up to my knees. Had we had more time to scurry, we probably could have taken cover in some deeper clumps or some depression, but time we did not have. We had barely moved back from the trail by two hundred paces when the Spaniards spotted us.

They must have been in a hurry to get to the herd of cattle because they had been galloping all along. Under those circumstances, continuing to run was unwise: it would only mark us as suspicious. I ordered my group to stop and catch a breath.

"Everyone! Conceal your weapons!" I said. "It is better they don't see that we are armed."

"And the bows? The javelins?"

"Hold them in hands, but carelessly, like a wandering bunch of Indians not expecting trouble."

I hid my musket in the grass next to where I was standing and hid the pistol in my waistband. I was naked like all my Indians and nearly as dark as they with all the sun exposure I have had. I now quickly covered my head with a red scarf, in a sailor's fashion, so that the riders would not see my blond hair. Several Indians wore similar scarves on their heads, so I didn't stand out. I had no beard either, for, having found a razor on the schooner, I had started shaving every day.

Overall, I looked quite like an Indian, just a tad on the fair side.

When the riders approached us to within a quarter of a mile, they slowed down as if in hesitation, then turned towards us. They came quite close, inspected us with interest, exchanged a few words amongst themselves, and... galloped off towards the herd.

They were a good hundred paces away when one of them must have said something to the others because they turned their astonished eyes on us. But despite this, they did not stop but continued on towards the cattle.

"Seven," said Vagura. "Will they come back?"

"It's possible," I said. "They looked at us as if they discovered something peculiar!"

I ordered my men to resume our march perpendicular to the cattle trail to get away as far as possible from the undesirable company. But it wasn't much help. On the flat *llanos*, in the clear air, one could see for miles around, and to run on foot from men on horseback was not going to work. I was still hoping that they would leave us in peace, but I was soon disappointed. The riders, having overtaken the herd, turned it around and began to drive the cattle towards us.

They rushed furiously, so the space between us shrank fast. At most, half an hour passed before they caught up with us and, leaving the herd a few hundred paces away, rode right up. We stopped like the first time, our firearms concealed, our native weapons held carelessly.

We laid our baggage on the ground.

"*Buenos dias!*" one of the newcomers greeted us gruffly—a huge Spaniard with a black beard and the appearance of a conquistador. Tucked in his belt, I saw a splendid pistol with a silver handle thickly encrusted with precious stones. He was probably their ringleader.

"*Buenos dias!*" several of us replied meekly.

The riders approached our group so close that their horses' heads almost touched ours. They looked at us with the sort of curiosity with which one inspects farm animals. In their lengthy silence and evaluating glances, one sensed contempt and a total lack of interest in us as men—an attitude born out of the deeply ingrained sense of the superiority of masters over slaves. Interestingly, there was an Indian among them: he looked at his kinsmen with the same haughty superiority as the rest of the Spaniards. Dressed like the others in pants and shirt, he held a long whip in his right hand. Black circles had been tattoed around his eyes, giving his face a monstrous and frightening expression. All the riders sported bushy beards except for the Indian and the youngest of the Spanish, a boy in his teens, who—wonder of wonders!—though a Spaniard, looked at us differently: with the open curiosity of someone who had not seen the natives in the wild.

Each of the riders wielded a long lance, evidently intended for prodding cattle. Four had fowling pieces strapped to their saddles, three—swords at their sides, and all—as I counted carefully—had pistols in their belts. They were armed up to their teeth, in other words, and all the more dangerous as four of their seven pistols were double-barreled and so could kill two opponents each.

"You see the Indian?" whispered Manauri to me. "He's a Cumanágoto."

"How do you know?"

"That tattoo around his eyes. His tribe do that."

"These men must be from *La Soledad*?"

"I am sure of it."

At last, their leader, that fellow with a silver gun, broke off his silent gaze and asked brusquely:

"Where are you going?"

He asked in Spanish, naturally, but it was easy enough for me to understand his intent.

"Beyond the Orinoco," replied Manauri truthfully. "We're going to the Pomeroon. Our home is there."

"And what are you doing here, in the north?"

"We lived for many years near Mount Vulture, but now we want to rejoin our tribe."

The answer, as truthful as the first, seemed to satisfy the bearded man. For all that, he did not move off but stared at us intensely, like a dog staring at a bone.

"What do you have in these bags?" he asked suddenly.

"Food."

"And what else?"

"Some small things."

"What things?"

"What things?" repeated Manauri without haste. "Just the things every Indian needs, gourds, ropes..."

"Oh, yeah? So... what do you have there?" insisted the Spaniard, pointing to Manauri's sack, without raising his voice but a little more insistently. I could feel impatience building up in him.

Just then, the Cumanágoto swung his whip wide and brazenly cracked it just above our heads. He did not strike anyone, but the cracking was so sharp that the children burst into tears.

"And this? What's this?" said the Spaniard and used the top of his lance to poke one of the bundles lying on the ground.

We looked down: an insufficiently concealed handle of a shovel poked out of it.

"This," explained Manauri patiently, "this is a tool for digging in the ground."

"And you need that every day? You, Indians? Such a rare piece of equipment?"

"Yes, sir. We are Arawaks."

"What does that have to do with anything?"

"We are farmers," explained the chief.

"And where did you get this shovel?" His voice sounded sharp now. "Where did you steal it?"

"We did not steal it."

"Oh? Did it fall from the sky?"

"No, it did not fall from the sky," continued Manauri, as calm as before. "It came from the sea."

I admired his tremendous presence of mind and his masterful composure, even if they were beginning to irritate the Spaniard.

"From the sea?" growled the bearded man. "Are you mocking me?"

"I would not dare mock you, sir!" said Manauri, as if alarmed. "An English ship ran aground near our lagoon. There was a storm. Many objects washed up on our shore."

"And these scarves, too, have come from the sea?"

Suddenly, the Spaniard, openly angry, raised his lance as if he intended to run Manauri through.

Manauri did not bat an eye. Quick, too quick, I gripped the butt of my gun. Luckily, none of the riders noticed. The Spaniard did not strike but shouted:

"You lying scoundrel! These scarves are fresh. They have never seen seawater!"

"You say true: they never have."

"So, did you lie?"

"No. I did not lie."

"Do I look stupid to you? Or are you stupid?"

Manauri remained calm, in perfect control.

"I am not trying to offend you, sir," he explained. 'I'm just telling you how it was that we found these scarves dry. They were in a chest, and the chest was watertight. It was washed up by the sea after the shipwreck... That's all, sir. That's it!"

Unfortunately, this was not all, for the trouble was only beginning. The bearded man continued:

"When did this happen? This shipwreck?"

"Not long ago. Three months, maybe. Maybe four."

At this point, the Spaniard directed his gaze to the side, where our African comrades stood, and boomed:

"And those over there, who are they?"

I now realized that the whole business had been about them from the very beginning.

"These people belong to our tribe," replied Manauri with the most indifferent expression.

"Your slaves?" the Spaniard furrowed his eyebrows. "Since when do you Indians keep slaves?"

"We do not keep slaves," said Manauri. "These are free people, and they belong to our tribe like the rest of us."

"Ah! Silly me! These are Indians! Of course! How could I have missed it?" exclaimed the bearded man. "They just had a little too much sun?"

"No, sir. They are black. But they have stopped being Africans and have become Arawaks."

The Spaniards greeted his words with an explosion of laughter.

"Stop playing a fool!" he rebuked Manauri. "Enough of fun and games. Tell me the truth, or we'll cut you all down! What hacienda did these slaves escape from?"

"Didn't I tell you, sir, that an English ship was wrecked near our coast?" said Manauri with an air of humble reproach.

"And these people survived the shipwreck, you say?"

"Yes, sir!"

"From the English shipwreck?"

"Yes!"

The Spaniard hesitated for a moment, thought about something, then brought the horse closer to the group of Negroes, of whom there were six, including Dolores—and pulling out his pistol from his belt, he turned to the woman with great courtesy:

"Tell me, beautiful *señora*, what is your name?"

"Dolores," she replied.

"And on which hacienda did you serve?"

Dolores had never been the brightest candle, but now, paralyzed with fear and watching the hand waving the gun, she barely remembered what Manauri had said about the English ship, and she began to explain:

"I was on the English ship, sir... I saved myself by swimming."

"And did your black companions come with you on the ship?"

"Yes, sir! Just so!"

"And was it an English ship, or was it a Spanish ship?"

"English, sir! English!"

"And have you never been in Spanish service?"

The terrified woman was at her wits end, but she bravely soldiered on:

"No, never!"

The Spaniard fell silent. After a moment's silence, he asked in the voice of a kindly teacher speaking to a pupil who had not learned her lesson:

"Then tell me, Dolores, where did you learn such beautiful Spanish?"

The woman, driven into a corner, began to sob, unable to speak.

And now the Spaniard turned to Manauri, still waving his gun as if playing with it. I didn't take my eyes off him for an inkling of an eye: I decided to put a bullet in his head the moment he pulled his pistol's cock. He had no idea, the conceited madman, that his life now hung by a thread.

"And you, who taught you your Spanish?" boomed the giant. "What's your name?"

"Manauri."

"And where did you learn your Spanish?"

"A missionary *padre* taught me. He lived in our village for a long time."

"So you're a Christian?"

"Yes, of course."

"Then cross yourself."

Manauri genuflected.

"In the name of the Father and the Son and the Holy Spirit."

Manauri knew how to do this. All the slaves on Margarita had had to adopt the religion of their masters.

"All right!" announced the Spaniard. "You, *Indios*, are free and go. But these five blacks and this woman stay with us. I claim them as runaway slaves."

"But sir!" exclaimed Manauri in a pleading voice. "They are not slaves! They have been accepted into our tribe. They are our brothers!"

"They are slaves, I say!" boomed the bearded man. "And if you're life is dear to you, you better hold your tongue."

Manauri winced as if scared by the threat.

Seeing such humility, I became terrified. I remembered how, very recently, my Indian friends fought the Spanish. I learned then that they were brave warriors ready to go against the devil himself. I did not expect such abject subservience from them. They stood there now in a docile, hulking heap, as if numb with fear, poor creatures, haggard, cowered by the screams of the imposing Spaniard, unable to raise their eyes, let alone their hands. Have their souls not yet shaken off the yoke of captivity? I became afraid—not of the enemy, but of our weaknesses, for I began to doubt whether they would strike when I gave them the command to attack.

Arnak and Vagura I could count on, I thought: they were tried and tested friends of many months. Surely, they at least would not fail me. I looked at them with apprehension, but I could read nothing in their faces—nothing except concentration and enigmatic passivity. Would they leave me in the lurch?

Meanwhile, the situation was becoming precarious, and a thick sense of impending violence hung in the air.

"They're our people!" Manauri pleaded for the Africans with a hint of despair. "Please, do not take them! We belong together! They are free people! Do not break up our tribe!"

"There are no free Africans in New Spain!" shouted the Spaniard. "They speak Spanish, so it is clear that they were slaves on a Spanish hacienda and ran away. Take them!" he ordered his men.

The riders approached the Africans and began to prod them with their lances away from the rest of our group. Dolores raised an inhuman, drawn-out scream.

"We must kill them all," I whispered to Arnak.

He blinked his eyelids to indicate that he heard me.

"Tell everyone to be ready."

"They're ready," said Arnak.

I was not convinced of that, but there was no time for taking a poll. I said to Arnak:

"Watch me!"

Meanwhile, the commotion about the Africans was getting serious. I stepped forward and cried:

"Stop!"

I shouted in English, of course, because I had no Spanish, but it worked. A commanding, booming voice, issuing for the first time out of our cluster of submissive, frightened Indians, surprised the riders, confused them, and they froze in amazement. They looked at me dumbfounded that an Indian had dared to raise his voice at them.

Only after a moment did their ringleader overcome his astonishment and turn to me in a voice thick with both anger and amusement:

"And you? What sort of mongrel are you?"

For me to understand, Manauri translated his words into Arawak and Arnak from Arawak into English. Filtered through their lips, the Spaniard's words reached me in a more decent and less offensive form.

"I am an Englishman, shipwrecked on this shore," I explained. "My name is John Bober."

"What a delightful encounter, Mr. English!" drawled the Spaniard, tucking his pistol away and lifting the edge of his hat in a greeting. "A do you have any idea where the devil has blown you? What country this is?"

"It is Venezuela, I suppose."

"You guessed right. This is Venezuela. And therefore, part of the Kingdom of Castile. As an Englishman, you are an honored guest in our country, of course, but you come uninvited."

"Fate has brought me here, not my choice."

"Who the devil knows how you came here? Anyway, what sort of an Englishman are you? Naked, feral like any *Indio*, even barefoot, without shoes?"

"Ah, yes, well, it is more comfortable this way. In any case, I do have shoes, look!"

I pointed to the boots, which I had donated to Arasibo. He had long since given up hobbling about in them, finding it easier to walk barefoot like the rest of us, but he never gave them up and still carried them on his back.

Apparently, the sight of the boots made a solid impression on the Spaniard, for he started on a different tack:

"And what have you just shouted at us? 'Stop?' Were we harming you?"

"You wanted to take my people."

"These blacks are your slaves?"

"No, but they are under my care."

"I don't get it."

"I have care of them, but they do not belong to me."

"Why? Do you represent their owner?"

"No. They have no owner. They are free members of the Arawak nation."

"Then I should do you the courtesy, *señor*, of informing you that what you are saying is pure hogwash. This is New Spain. There are no free Africans here. There *can* be no free Africans here. It is legally impossible. Furthermore, these blacks had clearly once been Spanish property, and back to Spanish hands they shall now return."

"No, *señor*, they will not—unless by an act of kidnapping on your part."

"Kidnapping? Are you calling me a kidnapper? Are you trying to offend me in my own country?"

"As God is my witness, no. I am being as courteous as you are."

I had heard much about the famous Spanish courtesy and hospitality, especially towards foreigners, sometimes even towards Indians. The bearded man stared at me gloomily. He was so conceited and self-assured that he didn't even sense the insult implied by my words.

"I would like us to part in mutual respect and understanding," I continued.

"I have said that these *Indios* are free to go where they like. You are free to go with them, too, if you like, or come with us and be my honored guest."

"I am speaking about the Africans."

"The Africans are another matter. I am taking them, and that's that. There is no use talking about it."

"*Señor*, if you do not wish to show us the famous Spanish magnanimity, then please, at least, do not be deaf to another famous Spanish virtue."

"And what virtue would that be?"

"The voice of common sense."

"Common sense?"

"Yes, common sense. Count us, *señor*. There are many more of us than there are of you. If it should come to acts of anger, surely we could easily overpower you. I recommend that we do not go there. Let us part amicably. Please tell your men to back off and leave our African brothers alone."

I said it calmly and politely, imitating the natural reserve of my Indians. I really wanted to avoid a fight. I was not certain that my men would fight, and I was eager to avoid suffering casualties in our group.

But the Spaniard only snorted in mockery at my words, taking my warning as an empty threat. Convinced of his superiority of arms and courage, the thought of serious resistance on our part did not enter his head.

"You presumptuous intruder!" he shouted outraged. "Not only have you illegally entered this kingdom, but you dare to threaten the King's subjects with violence? Well, I was not planning to arrest you, but I changed my mind. You, too, will come with us!"

"I will most certainly not go anywhere with you. I believe you are letting your anger get the better of you. I entreat you, come to your senses, *señor*."

But my words were in vain. He neither listened nor heard.

"To him!" he commanded his men and spurred his horse towards me.

His hand was free now, for he had tucked his pistol in his belt while we talked. Jumping towards me, he reached with his right hand, trying to take me by the scruff of my neck, but he didn't make it. I was faster: I pulled out my pistol, pulled the cock, and fired right into his face from a distance of no more than three feet. I had never done such a thing, and what I now saw made a huge impression on me. Though it lasted but a split second, the whole scene unfolded so slowly as if somehow time had frozen: my gun spat fire into the Spaniard's face, a great red flower bloomed in his right eye, and then his head opened up like a busted watermelon. Before I lost sight of him in the cloud of gunpowder smoke, I threw down my pistol, jumped for my musket, grabbed it, ran two paces forward while straightening up, turned around, and looked back to find my next target.

But there was no target to shoot.

The enemy was gone.

It's hard to put into words what happened after my shot. It must have lasted seconds. Several pistols roared at once as if fired from a single barrel, arrows shimmered in the air, spears jabbed, clubs cracked. The sudden transformation of my meek Indian lambs into enraged cats was amazing, impossible, incomprehensible: it was a sudden leap from apparent timidity directly into an explosion of unrestrained violence. The riders did not even have time to reach for their weapons. Shot, stabbed, hacked, they all fell to the ground almost immediately, barely uttering a wheeze.

Only one, the Cumanágoto, managed to dodge the missiles, spur his horse, jump right ahead through the midst of us, and gallop off into the steppe. But he did not get far: Miguel, a master javelin thrower, hurled his point after him, and it punched into the man's back with a terrible force and a sickening slurping sound. It ran the man right through and knocked him off his horse. Others jumped to him and clubbed him to death.

And it was all over. A moment of deafening silence. I stood still, stunned by the mad turn of events and even more by the skill and speed with which my comrades had done their job. We were indeed a fine detachment of warriors, and few others could have matched our efficiency and speed. Looking at my men with unfeigned admiration, I realized how much strength and how much unity of purpose resided in our troop and how unfairly I had judged them a moment ago, not trusting their courage! At the head of such fighters—there were twenty-one of them—I may yet achieve great things in this vast land!

Some of the horses met the fate of the riders and lay dead or dying on the ground, but the Indian's mount, having gotten rid of its encumbrance, was galloping away. Miguel, without thinking, jumped on one of the surviving horses and went after the fugitive. He knew how to ride a horse, a dashing young man, and soon brought the steed back, leading him by the reigns.

"You did well, *amigo*!" I jumped up to him with joy and shook his hand. "You stuck him on a stick and didn't even lose the horse!"

"Ha!" laughed Miguel. "I thought I owed it to you since you so boldly stood up in our defense! This horse is my gift to you!"

"There will be no traces of the Spaniards left!" said Manauri contentedly. "Nobody got away alive to betray us, not even a horse!"

"What now?" I asked him through Arnak.

"First, we bury them. And deep, too, so that the vultures do not dig them up and lead other Spaniards here."

"And then?"

That was the question: what next? After what had just

happened, was it safe to continue through the *llanos* as before? Would we not soon run into more Spaniards? Would the Spaniards of *La Soledad* not send out a search party for their missing men by nightfall at the latest? Under such circumstances, continuing with our march did not seem wise. And therefore, should we not return hurriedly to the lagoon and proceed on the schooner instead? We were less likely to meet Spaniards at sea than on land. Yes, it seemed the only way to proceed.

I did not fail to express my opinion to my companions at once, and this time, my suggestion did not encounter opposition. Everyone realized that wandering further through the open steppe was asking for trouble. They preferred to entrust their fate to the sea.

A moment later, as we began to dig the grave, an unexpected thing happened. One of the Spaniards, obviously not hit hard enough, regained consciousness. It was the bare-faced teenage youth who had looked at us with such curiosity. He now moved his hands and lifted his head. When my companions saw this, some of them rushed forward to club him to death. But I outran them and got to him before they did.

"No! No! Don't kill him!"

"Why not?" they shouted indignant. "He is a nasty, hateful Spaniard!"

"Yes, he is a Spaniard. Yes!" I said. "This is why we need him!"

"Need him? What for?"

"He will tell us what we need to know about the Spanish in this country. We must know what he knows!"

There was no use citing other causes, more humane ones, for sparing him. Besides, I was not exactly lying: the young man looked intelligent, and I assumed he would know a lot of useful things.

But my Indians were in a killing frenzy and behaved like wolves from whose mouth I had snatched a tasty piglet.

"Kill him! Kill him!" they demanded.

As had become traditional in all those situations, Arnak and Vagura took my side, and this time, so did the African Miguel. The three bravely stood by me. And then Manauri began to speak, appealing to reason. Finally, the bloodthirsty men relented, convinced by Manauri's argument that the young Spaniard should be my share of booty from the fight.

Besides, we all knew we had no time to waste on arguments. Soon, our four shovels went to work, we took turns every few minutes, and the work went lightning-fast.

Within two hours, we completed the job, and the men and their horses lay in the pit, covered by six feet of earth.

Even before we finished the job, several Indians wanted to take a calf for a supply of fresh meat.

"No!" I said. "Let us not waste time!"

"What will we eat, then?"

"Why, we have three horses! We will take them with us!"

The horses proved very useful: we loaded our prisoner, still dazed, on one and most of our bundles on the others. It was easier to walk unencumbered, so we made fast progress. Only Lasana, burdened with a small child, was struggling. She neither could nor wanted to go on horseback. Seeing how heavy the child was, I offered her help carrying it. She laughed:

"You want to carry my child?"

"What is so strange in that?"

"This is a woman's job, not a man's!"

"Stuff and nonsense!" I said, reaching my hands for the baby.

"The men will laugh at you! White Jaguar carrying someone's baby!"

The thing was so inappropriate to the minds of the Indians that those who walked near us and heard the conversation were amused and began to chuckle. But I paid no attention to their jokes and only worried about the woman and the child: we were half-running now.

"Give it to me!" I ordered Lasana and took the bundle off her back.

Lasana was both embarrassed and glad. In her eyes, I saw

something like boundless astonishment.

# Firearms

The next day, as the sun dipped low over the horizon, we returned to the lagoon under Mount Vulture. We found everything as we had left it: the deserted village, the hidden schooner, our cache secreted in the cave. We were in a hurry to get away from the place, so, despite our exhaustion, we immediately hauled the ship back out into the lagoon and began to load our possessions. The horses were the worst. We had great difficulty pulling them on board. With a tremendous effort, we finally managed to transfer them onto the ship, but the animals kicked viciously, and two of them broke their legs. This was no great loss because we planned to eat them on our journey anyway. In the evening, there was a heavy but short-lived rainfall, which we greeted with great relief: it would erase our traces on the steppe and would make a pursuit unlikely.

The young captive came to, so the Indians bound his hands and feet, and I assigned one to keep an eye on him. I assured the young Spaniard, saying that, for the moment, his life was in no danger, but he watched our preparations with increasing alarm. He saw us transfer firearms from shore to ship, and the sheer quantity of our weapons seemed to frighten him. As if he had only now awoken to the seriousness of his position, he began to cry, and his cries sounded sometimes like a complaint and sometimes like a threat.

"What does he want?" I asked.

"He wants to talk to you."

"Why me?"

The horses were already loaded, and the men were bringing stacks of freshly cut grass onto the ship, so I had a moment to spare. I summoned Manauri and Arnak to translate my conversation with the prisoner.

"What's your name?"

"I am Pedro Martinez y Gonzaga."

"You live on *La Soledad*?"

"Yes, sir."

"Your people oppress Indians. You saw yourself how they treated us."

"I saw it. But I have never done anything against Indians."

"Sure. I believe you."

"I say it because it is true!" he assured me in a trembling voice, with helpless despair in his eyes. He seemed sympathetic.

"Do you work on the ranch?"

The captive hesitated.

"Actually... I don't work there."

"So what do you do there? Spit and catch?"

"I was a guest at my uncle's house."

"Your uncle?"

"Yes. The owner of the ranch."

"I see. And if you do not work there, then how do you make your living?"

"Nowhere yet, *señor*. I am a student."

"A student? How old are you?"

"Eighteen. I study at the *Collegio* of the Dominicans."

"In *La Soledad*?"

"No, no. *La Soledad* does not have a school. In the city of Cumaná. I hope to become a doctor."

Pedro really looked like a man with some education, and I felt reassured in my original expectation that he may prove useful. The boy was a valuable prize.

Meanwhile, he watched me with confusion and a frozen expression of terror on his face.

"*Señor*!" he exclaimed with a choked voice. "What do you want of me? What will you do to me?"

"I will not do anything to you," I assured him. "You are my

prisoner. You will come with us."

"And who are you? Are you a pirate that you go out to sea?"

"Yes, we are going to sea, but no, we are not pirates. Do not be afraid."

"You are not pirates?"

"No."

"But you are an Englishman, sir. You have so many guns, you have a fast ship..."

"Nevertheless, we are not pirates."

"So where will you take me? To the islands of the English?" he asked fearfully.

"No, not to the islands. But I will not tell you where. This you will find out later while we are at sea."

Suddenly, his face changed, and again, he seemed close to crying.

"*Señor*!" he groaned. "Be compassionate. Let me go! Give me back my freedom, please! I haven't done anything wrong to you!"

"Yes, Pedro, this is true. You have not done anything wrong; your comrades did. But never mind that. Now listen! You are my captive, and you will remain so for months. You will teach me Spanish, that's why I need you. Then I will release you and send you to your own people. If you resign yourself to your present fate, I will show you kindness, give you my protection, and not a hair will fall from your head. But if you are difficult or try to run, I cannot vouch for your life. My friends wanted to kill you, and they will be very eager to do it."

We spent the night on shore, having set up sentries. Nothing untoward happened, and, refreshed by a few hours of sleep, we rose before dawn. The moon shone in the dark sky, but the stars were turning pale, heralding the coming of dawn. We cast off, dragging our three boats behind us, and began to feel our way towards the mouth of the lagoon.

It went smoothly, for the Indians knew the lagoon well. By sunrise, we were already at sea, catching the first gusts of the morning breeze. A mild northeaster filled our sails. We resumed our course along the coast, heading straight east as we expected to sail for several days.

Oh, the fleeting mutability of human feelings! The rough boards of the deck seemed to us our dearest friends and the schooner our native home. The smell of the sea seemed to us the scent of freedom. Friendly waves lapped at our sides, and a favorable wind filled us with good hope.

When our sails were all set up, the wind settled, and the schooner began to fly, I summoned all my companions around to hear what I had to say.

"I am grateful to you for the trust you have shown me, and I am proud of your friendship," I said. "It fills me with great pride that we make such a well-coordinated and brave team. How brilliantly we won the engagement on the *llanos*, how efficiently we destroyed that bunch of Spanish scum! My heart rejoices to think of it! But it is not certain that victory will follow us in the future as well. Our first encounter with the people in this land has warned us that this is a cruel and merciless place and that if we do not want to die, we must be strong, very strong, and very resilient!"

"True! True!" exclaimed Chief Manauri.

"We now have many firearms in our hands," I went on, "and plenty of gunpowder and lead! But what is the use of all this wealth when so few of us know how to shoot and handle guns? Apart from me, we have only two proficient shooters, Arnak and Vagura, but almost forty guns and as many pistols. What's the conclusion?"

"We must all learn to shoot!" said Arnak.

"Exactly! Every one of us should become a sharpshooter, and this as soon as possible. We should learn now, already, today, while we are still at sea. We should use every day of calm weather for practice."

The benefit of such learning was beyond any doubt, and Manauri accepted my idea with zeal. But many Indians, to my surprise, did not share the chief's opinion.

"Why would we need guns?" many voices said. "We'll soon reach the Pomeroon, and over there, among our own people, we will be safe. There, we can survive easily as we always have, with bows and clubs."

"But will they be enough?" argued Arnak. "Maybe yes, maybe no! There are still many days of uncertain travel before us, and it could be that many dangerous adventures still await us."

"You say that over at the Pomeroon," Manauri said, "nothing will threaten us anymore? Why, the Spaniards are spreading everywhere! Look, *La Soledad* came here only two years ago! There are more of them every day, and who knows if they are not already at the Pomeroon? And they are stronger than us! Why are they stronger than us? Because they have better weapons—matchlock bullets kill better than bow and arrows!"

"But not in the forest!" someone shouted.

"Maybe not in the forest. But we are not really a forest people! Where our villages lie, there lies open cultivated land, and the forest has retreated."

Wanting to put an end to the argument, I asked for silence.

"In my opinion," I declared, "the opinion of a man who has seen a lot of the world and wishes you good fortune from the bottom of his heart, there is no doubt that bows are useful in dense forests. But Manauri and Arnak are correct: it's always better to know how to use various weapons, especially firearms if you do not want to lose your freedom or your life. It's the oldest saying in the world that he who wields better weapons wins."

Still, there were those who did not want to learn. Here I was suddenly faced with a striking feature of the Indian psyche, familiar to me from those days when I was in North America, in the Virginia woods—namely, the reluctance to change, the refusal to believe that the future will not be like the past. They have lived in their way for generations, and they could not see—they refused to see—that everything was changing. But everything was changing—and fast.

Apart from Manauri, there were only five Indians willing to learn, and all, except Arasibo, were his personal friends. And even the poor invalid volunteered for personal reasons: he remembered that I showed pity for him and refused to abandon him under Mount Vulture, so he felt that he needed to support me in all my projects. The rest of the Indians on the ship preferred to remain idle. But one more person volunteered: Lasana.

"You? You want to shoot?" I stared at her with surprise.

But Manauri explained to me that many Indian women accompanied their husbands on war expeditions and used weapons, especially bows, very effectively. There was even a tribe on the river Cuyuni composed entirely of women warriors.

"That tribe is doomed to die out," observed Vagura tongue in cheek, showing off his profound understanding of certain fundamental facts of nature. "Without men..."

"Look what a wise man we have among us!" the chief nodded with pretended amazement, shooting the young man a maliciously approving look. "But in fact, it is a very militant tribe and constantly raids its neighbors to seize their children. They sometimes take men as slaves, too. And if one of their women knows such a slave and a girl is born, they release the captive, but if a boy, then they kill the child, and the man must continue to serve."

"That's cruel!" said Vagura, but, contrary to his words, his eyes slipped into a kind of a daydream.

The five Africans, meanwhile, kept whispering amongst themselves. Ever since the battle on the island, they were always eager to support me, and especially now, since the fight on the *llanos*.

And now, seeing the reluctance of the Indians to follow my lead, the Africans came up to me in a group, and Miguel said:

"We are all with you, Yan. We want to shoot muskets. So you have twelve students now. Let us begin."

There was no better time than now. Using the captured pistol with a silver handle—what a beauty that was!—I showed them how to load a gun, how much powder to put, and how much lead. The lesson was not entirely new to them, for, over the last few days, they have had a chance to see matchlocks in action.

After this introduction, Arnak and Vagura took over further

instruction.

The wind was constant, and an experienced Indian stood at the helm. When the young captive, Pedro, saw me unoccupied, he came forward and offered to teach me Spanish. He was no longer bound, was free to move about the ship, and was gradually growing more sure of himself. We now sat in the shade of an awning and began our first lesson. He first touched his head and said: *la cabeza*. Then he raised his hand and said: *la mano*. He pointed to the ship: *el navio*. And so began my study.

Pedro was a bright young man. He taught clearly, and after an hour, I had absorbed some useful vocabulary. When the men tinkering with the guns were taking a break, I summoned Arnak and Manauri and told them to ask Pedro if he had studied the geography of South America. Of course, he had, he said. Had he seen its maps? Especially of our area? Of course, he had. Could he draw it from memory, especially this part of the coast? He wasn't sure, but he said he would try.

We had found many valuable objects on the ship, including paper, and ink, and pens. I now ordered them brought up, and asked Pedro to try to draw the coastline of this part of South America.

The young Spaniard first traced the contours lightly with a piece of lead and corrected what he thought was distorted, then drew with ink. We stared at his fingers like enchanted and the Indians— with bated breath. Vagura, Miguel, and Lasana joined us.

The coastline ran straight eastward, more or less hundred twenty miles, then cut deep inland, making a bay, and then turned southeast and ran so until the end of the paper. In the place of its bending lay the great island of Trinidad, as if blocking the gulf from the ocean and making a kind of immense lagoon or lake, with two outlets to the sea, one to the north and one to the south. *Golfo de Paria* Pedro wrote across the lagoon: the Gulf of Paria.

"And where is the mouth of the Orinoco?" I asked.

"The main mouth?" asked the Spaniard.

"Yes, the main one," I replied, though I had had no idea that there was another.

The main mouth was farther south, about a hundred and fifty miles from the island of Trinidad, and the Orinoco itself flowed from the interior in an almost straight line from west to east. But about a hundred and fifty miles from the sea, numerous branches of the river began to break away northward, some flowing into the Gulf of Paria opposite the island of Trinidad, others into the open sea. The great number of these channels formed among them a great multitude of islands, and Pedro called this land the Delta of the Orinoco. I had been proud of my education—for I had learned when I was still a boy to read and write and have read several books, but—oh misery!—how meager was my knowledge of the world! And now, before my eyes, on the white sheet of paper, Pedro conjured up mysterious landmarks, rivers, islands, bays—all of which were a great novelty to me.

In fact, the Indians turned out to be more enlightened in this matter because they read Pedro's lines easily and confirmed the fidelity of the map with a murmur of appreciation.

"Now, draw the islands of the English in the Caribbean Sea," I said.

Pedro made a confused expression and declared that Jamaica lay too far in the northwest, beyond the reach of our sheet of paper.

"I mean Barbados, not Jamaica," I explained.

Barbados lay directly to the north of Trinidad, he said, but too far to fit on our map, two hundred miles from land.

"Are you sure?"

"Yes, *señor*. I am sure."

That was not close, and I thought with some anxiety how difficult it would be to get there. Meanwhile, the Indians demanded to see the Pomeroon River. Pedro said it was a small river, so he did not know its exact position by heart, but he knew that it lay to the south of the Orinoco, between the Orinoco and the outlet of the next great river, the Essequibo.

"Yes! That is true!" exclaimed Manauri.

Pedro drew the mouth of the Essequibo about two hundred miles to the southeast of the mouth of the Orinoco, and the Indians have confirmed the accuracy of his drawing by marking the course of the river Pomeroon about fifty miles to the north of Essequibo.

And now I stared at that map, lost in thought. It opened before my eyes a little bit of this world, where an unknown fate awaited me in the coming months.

After a moment, Pedro interrupted the silence:

"Is there something else I must draw?"

We all hesitated. Then Vagura spoke up.

"Yes!" he said with great confidence.

But when Pedro asked him kindly what he wished to know, Vagura became a bit flustered, something wobbled in his eyes, and he answered not so firmly now, almost shyly:

"Show us the River Cuyuni."

"It is a left tributary of the Essequibo River," Pedro explained, and at the same time drew its supposed course on the map. "It flows like this. Like the Orinoco, east to west, through a dense and little-known forest. A powerful and warlike tribe of the Caribs, the Akawaio, lives on its lower reaches."

"Right again!" confirmed Manauri.

"And where is that other tribe? The ladies?" asked Vagura.

"I don't know."

For some time now, Manauri, Arnak, Lasana, and I had been exchanging amused glances, but now we couldn't help bursting out laughing.

"Why are you yelling like that?" scoffed the young would-be geographer. Shrugging his shoulders, he walked away. Usually cheerful, he was now terribly hurt and offended.

"And where are the cities of the Spanish on this map?" I asked Pedro, pointing to the lower Orinoco region on the map.

"I am not sure that I know them all," replied the young man. "There aren't many of them anyway. For example, there is a Spanish settlement on the island of Trinidad. I think it faces the Gulf of Paria.

On the Orinoco itself, I remember the settlement of Angostura,[5] one hundred and fifty or two hundred miles upriver from the mouth of the Orinoco."

"No others?"

"Spanish—maybe no. Not even small ones. But south of here are the Dutch. People say that the Dutch had penetrated deep inland and set up trading posts on the river Cuyuni. They got in some scrapes with the English there, who have factories at the Essequibo River."

"Pedro!" I broke out. "What did you say? English factories?"

"Yes... English trading posts... Yes, sir!... That's what I was told, but..." He stopped, somehow frightened, seeing the sudden change in my face.

"Are you not mistaken, my boy?"

"No, no. I am not mistaken. I have heard about the English there more than once."

"English factories at the mouth of the Essequibo?" I repeated, not believing my own ears.

"Yes, *señor*, at the mouth of the Essequibo."

The news hit me like lightning: English trading posts at the mouth of the Essequibo! Maybe fifty miles south of the Pomeroon, which was our objective. Ha! That could be the end of my wanderings in this foreign land! Could it be so easy to find a haven among my compatriots? In a sudden surge of joy, I was ready to hug Pedro and kiss all my companions, but when I cooled down from the first elation, doubts soon arose in my mind again.

"All of this is part of the Spanish Main," I said, "which the Spanish regard as their exclusive property since the days of the Spanish discoveries. Is it not so?"

"Yes, it is, señor."

"So how could the Dutch settle over here and the Dutch and the English over there without the permission of the Spanish? Did the Spanish government allow it?"

---

[5] Saint Thomas de Guyana, founded 1576, now Ciudad Bolívar.

"Oh, no!"

"So why don't the Spanish just throw them out?"

"Because they can't. Their power does not reach all that far, not all the way to Guyana."

"It does not reach that far?"

"No, no. It is too far from the main Spanish cities in Venezuela and Panama. And besides, between Venezuela proper and the area occupied by the English and Dutch, there is a vast wall of tropical forest, very difficult to pass. And many warlike tribes dwell in that forest. They have defeated and destroyed many Spanish expeditions. That's where the Akawaio live. Everyone is afraid of the Akawaio. So, for the time being, the Spanish gave up."

"And these Akawaio suffer the Dutch and the English gladly? Why won't they just cut their throats?"

"I have heard that the Akawaio live in peace with the Dutch. They are allies."

I must say, the picture presented by Pedro, despite its initial appearance of the fantastic, seemed likely: some Englishmen had to be sitting by the Essequibo River! This fundamentally changed my previous plan for my return to my homeland.

The conversation with Pedro had established another thing: the date. I'd had my timing completely messed up for years, but now I learned that the day on which the young Spaniard drew his map was the 12th day of September of the Year of Our Lord 1727. Learning this, I charged Pedro with the responsibility of keeping our calendar henceforward.


We anchored near the shore at night and, according to the established custom, raised anchor at dawn. On the following day, at about noon, I experienced a great emotion when I saw the dramatic change in the vegetation on the shore. Here suddenly ended the mostly sun-burnt scrub of cacti and grasses and thorny bushes, and a high-canopy forest began—extremely dense and tangled and dark green. It was the beginning of the Great Forest, that great impenetrable wilderness, hot, rich, full of green splendor, the child of the southern sun and steamy moisture. I couldn't take my eyes away from my spyglass, enchanted by the luxuriance of plant life. I, a staunch hunter, had only known the temperate forests of my cool homeland.

"Henceforth," explained Manauri, having noticed my interest, "henceforth, it will be forest and forest and forest. Nowhere will you see anything else but the same green everywhere!"

"Everywhere?"

"Everywhere. On the Essequibo and on the Pomeroon, and on the Orinoco, and everywhere in between, and also on the island of Kairi, which the Spaniards call Trinidad, and around the Gulf of Paria. The whole country is covered with one uninterrupted forest.


September in those parts marks the beginning of the dry season, which differs from the rainy season in that the downpours are not quite as heavy and a little less frequent, and there are fewer violent storms. Thanks to this, we had a generally gentle sea and a calm voyage. Thus, training with firearms took place regularly, whenever the heat allowed, every morning and every evening. The twelve, full of goodwill, made good progress while the rest, hard-set in their idleness, looked upon them with pity. But on the evening of the third day of the voyage, an incident took place that affected the recalcitrant idlers like the lash of a whip.

That evening, we dropped anchor a little earlier than usual, before twilight, and, as usual, some of our companions rowed ashore to gather feed for our last remaining horse. (The others had long since gone into our soup). Since it was still light, some of our men decided to hunt on land and, armed with bows and knives, entered the forest. They had been there less than half an hour when, suddenly, we heard loud screams from the forest.

"They were attacked!" exclaimed Manauri.

The screams came from several directions at once.

"Someone is chasing them!" boomed Arnak.

"Arnak!" I yelled. "Muskets! Into the boat! All hands to oar!"

Fortunately, we had a dozen loaded guns stored below deck and always at the ready. There was some confusion because so many threw themselves to fetch them, but I quickly organized them in a living chain.

Handing weapons from hand to hand went briskly, and soon, there were twelve guns in the larger boat. I jumped in and grabbed the oar. Behind me came Manauri and several others and—among them—Lasana. There was no need to hasten the men. They rowed so hard and fast that their eyes seemed ready to pop out of their heads. Arnak and several others followed in the smaller boat. The shore wasn't far away, fifty or sixty fathoms from the ship, but we barely made it at the last moment. Our hunters had just burst out of the forest onto the open sand and were rushing pell-mell towards us, while behind them came a whole swarm of Indians. There were dozens of them. They yelled at the top of their voices and shot from the bows as they ran.

I peppered them with lead shot from about a hundred paces. At that distance, the shot was not deadly, but it stung all the same. And just at that moment, at my side, boomed the second shot and the third, and the fourth, and then a few more all at once—a deafening volley. For the attackers, the lighting and thunder were enough. They came to a screeching halt, turned around on a dime, and disappeared into the forest. We did not lose a single man: only one was slightly wounded by an arrow. Fortunately, it was not poisoned.

"Who was that?" I asked.

"Pariagoto probably!" replied Manauri and added with disgust: "Damned Caribs."


Lasana was among those who fired a shot toward the shore. The woman had not had much practice shooting, so she forgot to hold the gun properly to her shoulder and got a solid kick in the arm and cheek. She was hurt, her lip was split and bleeding, but it wasn't dangerous.

"Now I am an experienced sharpshooter!" she exclaimed, covering with a self-deprecating joke her pain and confusion.

"Ho, ho! An experienced sharp-shooter!" I laughed, amused, and nodded my head. "And whom did you hit?"

"Can't you see? Myself!"

"Thank god you missed all of us!"

"Don't be so sure of yourself, White Jaguar! In the future, I might not miss you!"

She said it with such a strangely ambiguous expression that I wondered whether it was not a *double-entendre*.


Not wanting to expose ourselves to another attack, we took the ship out to sea and spent the night there. And when, on the following morning, as usual, Arnak and Vagura summoned their comrades to practice with guns, all men, without exception, volunteered to train. Nor was it but a brief enthusiasm. From then on, we all trained together, and our bond, forged by our common struggle, was strengthened by a new experience: the training in arms together. The future was to show how strong those bonds became.

The unpleasant adventure with the Pariagoto happened on the stretch of the coast named by Pedro the Peninsula of Paria, near the place where that peninsula ended just opposite Trinidad Island, and on the following afternoon, there opened before our eyes, the wide waters of the Bay of Paria. Here, we were supposed to turn and head south, but when we reached the tip of the peninsula, we found that a very strong current came out of the Gulf of Paria and that we were not able to make any headway against it. Whenever we tried, the strong current carried us north like a feather and flung us far out to sea.

*Boca del Drago*, the Spanish called it, Pedro explained to me: the Dragon's Maw. The current in the strait between the peninsula and Trinidad was so powerful that only the largest ships could beat it, and that supposedly only on certain days, for the strength of the current was variable.

"Why is the current so powerful?"

"Because the other, eastern opening of the bay, through which the current enters it, is much wider, and a great mass of water enters through it. That mass of water must find an exit through this narrow passage, only several miles across. Also, several branches of the Orinoco feed into the bay, increasing the pressure. All this squeezes together here, and the result is—*La Boca del Drago.*

There was no helping it, then: we could not hope to break through the current into the Bay of Paria with our light schooner. So, having given the nasty Dragon's Maw a respectable berth, we continued east, this time along the north coast of Trinidad. Going around the great islands extended our trip by more than a hundred miles, but the weather was in our favor, and we saw no Spanish nor any other ships. Nor did we see any trace of the natives, though every evening, we rowed ashore to collect horse fodder and fresh water. Finally, we reached the eastern tip of Trinidad. There, we turned our ship straight south, and after two day's sail along the eastern shore of the island, we saw the mainland again.

What a different landscape greeted us here! As far as the eye could see, it was a flat country with not the slightest hill or depression. This was the famous Orinoco Delta, more than two hundred miles wide, a land of innumerable forks of the river, broad lagoons, salt marshes and jungle, a land of thousands of islands, islands and islands and islands, and marshes between them. An eternal forest covered this land. Yes, in this, it was similar to the land of the Paraiagoto, but while there were mountains and hills there, here it was all low-lying swamp and mire. Endless miles and miles of jungle marched right down to the water's edge and—into it, hoisting themselves out of the surf on aerial roots, all tangled together in mad confusion.

"Surely, no people can live here?"

"Oh, but they do: the Guarauno!"

"Where do they live?"

Capuchin Monkeys

"On dry clumps within the Delta, or else on the water, in houses on stilts. They live by fishing."

The sea was now a different color. It had lost its navy blue clarity and had become cloudy and yellow with the mud and silt carried by the great river. It was as if from the great Orinoco emanated out into the ocean some great incomprehensible force which subdued everything before it. And while we sailed day after day past these endless swamps shrouded in inaccessible secrecy, we fell more and more under the spell of the ominous majesty of this vast wilderness.

We did not neglect our usual occupations on board: me learning Spanish and—still surreptitiously—Arawak and my comrades—the handling of firearms. By the time we reached the main outlet of the Orinoco, we formed, I felt, a close-knit group of friends and allies. None of us knew what awaited us in the near future, and this uncertainty bound us all into one harmonious group, as if a brotherhood, you could say: a newly formed tribe.

My comrades had made good progress in the difficult science of handling firearms, both shooting them and protecting them from damage in this merciless climate. What's more: they seemed to develop a fondness for their weapons. These muskets, fowling pieces, blunderbusses, and pistols became something dear and precious to them: objects of true affection.

Not wishing to create any misunderstandings or disappointments, I declared that the weapons belonged to me for the moment but that whoever proved that he could handle his gun well would eventually take possession of it.

Sailing along the Orinoco Delta was a challenge because of the lack of good drinking water, so when the vast view of the main estuary opened before our eyes, we decided to sail a little upstream, where we hoped to find fresh water more easily. It was high tide, the current was pushing inland, and we sailed briskly past one of the larger islands. After a couple of hours, we turned into a side branch of the river and dropped anchor near a thicket on a dry shore. Several men sent out to scout the area soon came back, running at full speed as if chased by demons. Already from the shore, they made urgent, silent signs of warning. As they scrambled hurriedly back into the schooner, they told us in a great panic that a great Indian settlement stood a short distance away in the jungle.

# Where Ants Are Judges

Mindful of the sad experience we had had on the Paria Peninsula, some of us rushed to their weapons, others prepared to raise the anchor. We stood very close to shore, hidden under the dense mass of branches which extended far above the surface of the water. We hoped that the local Indians hadn't noticed us and that we could at least get to the other side of the river before any attack took place.

But an attack did not take place even though the Indians did discover us. Instead, out of the dense bush right next to us, we heard a voice calling to us. The caller was perhaps no more than a dozen steps away, but we saw not a sign of him in the lush foliage. Nor did we understand a word he said. A moment later, we heard another cry from the canopy of the trees, almost directly overhead. We looked up and stared, but that speaker, too, remained invisible.

"These must be the Warao!" whispered Manauri fearfully.

"Warao or Guarauno is the same thing," explained Arnak.

Then we heard a third voice, and this stunned us into a complete stupor: the voice had come from the water itself, right at the bow of our ship.

There was no one in the river, and yet the sound was clearly coming from under our side. I knew of the existence of so-called ventriloquists, people with the extraordinary ability to send their voice from different directions, but I hadn't imagined they could do this sort of thing. The voices terrified us, and our position seemed extremely precarious. It is not nice to hear mysterious noises all around you, see no one, and expect to be pelted with a hail of arrows at any moment. The locals realized our confusion and, we knew perfectly well, were having fun at our expense. As we looked out over the water, trying to detect the source of the mysterious voice, we heard derisive laughter from several directions at once. Foreign words addressed to us were repeated again and again and sounded like a question—perhaps they were asking who we were.

So Manauri shouted a reply—first in Arawak, then in Spanish—that we were Arawaks, or Lokono because that's what Arawaks called themselves. The locals must have understood the word "Arawak" because they repeated it several times, as if making sure, then began to shout something, as if summoning someone from afar. After several minutes of silence, another voice spoke to us in a language we understood—in Arawak.

"Are you Arawaks?"

"Yes, we are Arawaks," shouted Manauri.

"What are you doing here?"

"We're on our way home. To the Pomeroon."

"Where are you coming from?"

"From the foot of Mount Vulture."

There was some silence in the thicket as if the man hidden there was thinking or consulting quietly with others. Then he shouted again, this time angrily:

"You are lying!"

"Why do you say that?"

"The Arawaks left Mount Vulture a long time ago. No one remained behind. You are not from Mount Vulture!"

The stranger was well-informed. No doubt he was Arawak, but from a different region than my companions.

"But we do come from Mount Vulture! Chief Manauri never lies, remember that!" replied the chief in a rebuking voice and briefly narrated the story of the Spanish attack at Mount Vulture and about his people's captivity on Margarita, their recent escape, arrival at Mount Vulture and the decision to travel to the Pomeroon.

"And you? Who are you?" he asked in the end.

"My name is Fujudi, and I come from the river Essequibo," replied the voice in a much friendlier tone.

"And what are you doing here, in the Orinoco, so far from the Essequibo?"

"I left Essequibo last dry season. I am visiting my friends, the Warao. I belong to the tribe of Chief Coneso. We live at the mouth of the river Imataca."

"Coneso? The one who was chief at Mount Vulture?"

"Yes, the same."

"And where are they now? They are just the people we are looking for!"

"Coneso is now on the Orinoco, not far from here."

"What did you say?! Didn't he go back to the Pomeroon?"

"No! It's too dangerous there. Too many Akawaio! Coneso first went there, then returned north and settled on the Orinoco at the mouth of the Imataca!"

"How far is that from here?"

"Five days upstream, four days downstream."

This news, so important to us, greatly affected everyone on the ship. There was no need to sail for the Pomeroon! Our objective was right here, on the Orinoco!

The previously talkative Fujudi, as he introduced himself, now fell silent, apparently passing our information to someone else. Now, new suspicions arose about us, for after a silence of many minutes, Fujudi asked:

"On your ship are not only Arawaks. Who are the others?"

"These black people are Africans who ran away from captivity with us and joined our tribe," Manauri explained.

"And this young *Espaniol*?"

"He's our captive. We wiped out a Spanish detachment and took him prisoner."

"You wiped out a whole detachment of Spaniards? Are you great heroes?"

It sounded like irony.

"Yes, we did. I can't help it. Whether you believe it or not, we did."

"So why did you take the captive?"

"He knows the country and knows where the Spanish are."

"And that other *jalanaui*?"

*Jalanaui* meant "white man."

"He is *Paranakedi* (English). He is a rich chief in his country, a famous hunter and warrior. He has a fearless heart, immeasurable experience, and is very cunning in war."

"*Ayayay!*"

"And he is a dear friend of ours. Thanks to him and his muskets, we won two great victories over the Spanish."

"*Ayayay!*"

"We killed them all and took this ship."

"And this horse?"

"And this horse! Our *Paranakedi* is a great war chief."

"What do you call this wonder?"

"What wonder?"

"This wonder of bravery, this *Paranakedi*?"

"We call him White Jaguar!" replied Manauri without a moment's hesitation.

I guessed that this excessive glorification of my person was not mere boasting: the chief had his reasons for it. He was as cunning as a fox, and by generously imbuing me with all sorts of qualities of power and all kinds of virtues, he was lending an aura of power to himself: the locals better not seek a quarrel with him, White Jaguar's friend! Manauri did not know how his native tribe may receive us, and he feared an unfriendly welcome—so he preferred to spread the word of our invincibility.

"And you say he is rich?" asked Fujudi, less taunting now, rather surprised. "Is this why he goes naked like the rest of you?"

There go the boots again! I thought. The natives could not imagine Europeans otherwise than dressed in thick layers of wool and leather, shod, behatted, and with a shiny sword at their side. In their minds, the notion of power was combined with sumptuous attire. A European without clothes was a jackass without authority or importance. And how could I explain to them that while on a deserted island, in a hot climate, I got used to wearing no clothes, feeling more comfortable without them?

"Such is his habit, and such is his whim!" Manauri said without batting an eye. "He is so powerful that he does what he wants, and no one can say anything about it!"

With this, a favorable opinion of us was finally established on shore. Fujudi called out that he wanted to come on board and that we should send a boat to pick him up. While he climbed into our launch, the great wall of dark greenery parted for a moment, and we caught a glimpse of a great multitude of Indians, bows in hand, hidden among the trees nearby. We would not have come out unscathed from any hostile confrontation.

Fujudi was a stocky, muscular man in his prime, with sharp but shifty eyes and lively movements. He was a brainy fellow, one could see that immediately in his eyes. For the first time in my life, I saw an Indian in a full ceremonial dress. He wore a crown of feathers and three rich necklaces about his neck, hung with various colored nuts, fish teeth, and animal horns.

Otherwise, he was quite naked, wearing only a loincloth, but his whole body—and especially his face—was richly adorned with black and red paint.

My comrades, dressed as they had escaped from captivity—in a few incongruous items of European clothing or nothing at all—were full of admiration—admiration bordering on envy—at the sight of this getup. And it seemed as if, in the presence of this properly decked-out dandy, they felt the first breath of freedom and only now fully realized the purpose of our journey.

With understandable eagerness, they inquired about the

current position of their compatriots at the mouth of the Imataca, but Fujudi answered them only grudgingly and half-heartedly that everything was all right, while he himself demanded a detailed description of our adventures. My comrades hid nothing. At length, Fujudi turned to me:

"My compatriots praise you, White Jaguar, and say that you have helped them and that you are their good friend. Therefore, I welcome you as a friend. May you be my brother, too. Jekuana, my host here, the chief of this branch of the Warao, invites you and all your friends to come to his village. He has a great celebration today and wants to celebrate it with you."

"We gladly accept his invitation," I replied. "And what is this great celebration?"

"It is the Judgment of the Ants. His oldest son is getting married today."

I had no idea what a Judgment of the Ants might possibly be, but my companions showed such cheerful excitement at the prospect that to ask would only spoil their fun. Then a dozen great boats came around the bend of the river, bearing many oarsmen, and rowed up to us. They hauled our schooner around the bend in the river and brought us to the Warao settlement, which lay very near, about a quarter of a mile as the crow flies.

Meanwhile, Manauri and Arnak brought me my Spanish uniform—that fancy, hellishly hot thing that I had never wanted to wear, and they told me to put it on. I decided to trust their knowledge of local manners, and though I hated the damn thing, I donned it properly. Also, I put on the boots, girded a mother-of-pearl-hilted sword at my side, and tucked the silver pistol in my belt. But the pinnacle of splendor and opulence turned out to be the jaguar skin.

Ah, now I understood why, over the last few days of our voyage, our women had taken the skin out on the deck of the schooner to air, rubbed it with coconut oil, and combed it until it glistened with a beautiful gloss. This was the skin of the jaguar that Arnak, Vagura, and I had killed on Robinson Island. Now, it was placed on me in such a way that the predator's head covered mine, leaving only my face exposed, and the rest of the skin hung loosely over my back and sides, reaching down to my feet. The effects of this masquerade proved to be absolutely riveting.

My companions looked at me as if I were some kind of a god, and the usually ironic eyes of Lasana became moist with a kind of elation, becoming devilishly alluring in the process. Something like vanity tickled my soul, but I checked it, embarrassed, and asked Manauri:

"Listen, chief! All is good, fun and games, and all. But can you vouch for these Warao? Could this be a trick to lure us into their camp and then maybe imprison us?"

"No, it is not a trick," Manauri and Arnak assured me. "Believe us!"

Meanwhile, we reached the village. In a clearing torn out of the screaming, screeching jungle, a dozen huts stood on stilts, with roofs of palm fronds but mostly without walls. Other homesteads were scattered here and there, at various remove from each other and the center of the village. In the middle of the clearing, which reached all the way down to the water, there was a vast upraised platform, also on stilts, about a hundred paces long and a hundred wide. There were a dozen huts upon it, close to one another, grander and larger than those scattered about the neighborhood. They surrounded an open space on three sides, creating an elevated courtyard open to the river.

And in that courtyard, under a large roof of palm fronds, the chief Jekuanua awaited us, surrounded by tribal elders and a dozen or so warriors armed with bows, javelins, clubs, and shields. The chief was a man of great bulk and sat on a richly carved stool while the rest stood about at attention. Nearby were three empty stools, probably meant for us, their guests.

All these people had their bodies painted, profusely adorned with necklaces, sashes, and strings of wild animal and colorful fruit. But only Jekuana wore a head plume, from which I concluded that the headdress was an emblem of chiefdom and that the Arawak Fujudi, dressed in the same manner, considered himself equal to the chief. As had been explained to me, the ceremonial required that Jekuana await us sitting on his stool and only rise and speak after we approached him.

But the chief, stunned by our appearance, was unable to contain himself or remain in his seat. Barely did we climb up the ladder onto the platform—I and a few companions, armed for greater effect with matchlocks (for the rest of us remained on the schooner guarding it and all our possessions)—when Jekuana, despite his obesity, jumped up from his seat with surprising agility and ran up to greet us.

His speech, translated by Fujudi into Arawak—fortunately not very long—was very cordial, and Manauri answered him just as politely. Under the roof, right by the stools, stood several enormous earthenware pots, each holding a good two hundred quarts and filled with a cloudy yellowish liquid. As Jekuana, Manauri, and I sat down, men began to scoop up the liquid with gourds and pass it around for us to drink. It was sour and stank to high heaven but was palatable and clearly contained alcohol.

"This is *kashiri*," whispered Arnak standing behind me, "a drink made with cassava. Don't drink too much!"

At the same time, we heard the rhythmic beating of many drums, and men and women, in two rows, came out into the courtyard before us. To the accompaniment of rather monotonous singing, they formed a circle and began to perform a languorous dance with slow and graceful hand movements. Their faces were sternly serious.

The dance was led by a man in a wooden mask representing some ghostly bogeyman. His dance was energetic and quite violent and depicted some kind of a hunting or battle scene.

"This is their sorcerer," explained Arnak.

I wondered: was this the fellow who had caused those strange, disembodied voices?

Jekuana was a peculiar Indian: he was not only distinguished by abundance of body but also by the extreme cheerfulness of his disposition. He smiled at everyone, especially us, his guests, he babbled, told humorous stories, and encouraged everyone to drink.

Gourds with *kashiri* were constantly circulating from hand to hand, but I took smaller and smaller sips, and finally, I only wet my lips. Despite this, completely unaccustomed to liquor as I was, I felt slightly dizzy and terribly hot. In the cruelly steamy air, sweat poured off me in streams, and not only off me—off everyone. At one point, in a fit of frustration and despair, I peeled off the jaguar's skin, threw it on the floor, and stamped on it passionately with my boot. I thought people would be outraged, but—no. On the contrary. Jekuana accepted my action with admiration, as a symbol of domination over the nature of the jaguar, and he cried out, clapping his hands:

"White Jaguar!... Our brother: White Jaguar!"

Encouraged by this, I stripped off my captain's uniform and just as vigorously trod upon it. The Indians, led by the same intuition, took this as a sign of my contempt for the Spaniards, and they rejoiced amid shouts:

"The tamer of the Spaniards! The killer of the Spaniards!"

Some of them immediately wanted to drag Pedro out and torture him, but I objected, and they left him in peace.

Meanwhile, in the courtyard in front of us, dancing and singing went on without a break, the general uproar growing by the minute. Slowly, the passionate mood of fun affected me. Bewildered by everything—the *kashiri*, the drums, the dancers, the stifling stuffiness of the air—I suddenly saw my presence among these Indians as fantastic and strange. Was it an accident, or was it Divine Providence that had brought me to this forest village at the mouth of a Venezuelan river? Was it really me, the Virginian John Bober, who laughed unthinkingly at fat Jekuana's jokes, watched the dancing Indians, noted with pleasure the coquettish smiles of the livelier girls, and absorbed—took into myself whole—the unfathomable strangeness of these people, so absurdly other and different, and yet so friendly?

Ah! The utter strangeness of these people. Yes! This unexpected intrusion of mine into this Warao ceremony, into the vortex of their intoxicated celebration, seemed like a fantastic but wonderful dream. And soon, another feeling followed—a cordial warmth. The Warao were strangers to me, it is true, but my traveling companions, bound to me by common fortune and misery, how close they were to my heart! They were so dear to me that I loved them like family. I experienced such a sense of community with them that they seemed to me like my fatherland. Ruled by this strong sense of attachment, I felt euphoric even amid the sheer oddity of this wonderful, foreign world.

And its wonders were amazing! For, suddenly, a large bird appeared right in front of me, a bird from a fairy tale, gigantic: a white stork with a black upturned beak. For some moments, it stared at me dumbfounded—I must have seemed as strange a monster to it as it seemed to me, and then it calmly began to devour the baked fish spread before me on broad banana leaves. The Indians laughed and drove it away; it immediately returned with sullen determination and continued stealing whatever came within reach of its beak. And then a dozen tame monkeys joined him and, glancing suspiciously at the freak that was me, wreaked havoc in my supply of sweet fruit. Countless domesticated birds and quadrupeds—most of which I had never seen before—were swarming between people's legs.

And then, the drums died down, with the exception of one. The dancers stopped and scattered. Where tall poles protruded from the platform, two small, elongated nets, which they called *hammocks*, were hung horizontally.

To them, two young people were now led: a boy the age of our Vagura and a much younger girl. I would have guessed her to be no more than thirteen years old, but her well-developed breasts showed that she was no longer a child.

They were the newlyweds. Dressed like most of the people— only in a fiber loincloth (she also sported a small apron covering her private parts) and, therefore, almost naked, they had to lie down in the two hammocks hanging side by side. The sorcerer, who meanwhile took off his mask and turned out to be an elderly, if lively, man with strangely disoriented eyes, danced around the hanging couple, shouting incantations over them and waving two small, tightly closed baskets. Though there was a great crowd of us—men, women, children—a complete silence fell in the village. Only the monkeys, chased away from their fruit, kept chirping from a distance.

I noticed that Jekuana, the groom's father, became serious and sober.

At one point, the sorcerer, still dancing, approached me and, in an act of special grace, allowed me to peek into one of the baskets by opening its lid for a moment: it was teeming with thousands of swarming, angry ants.

Then, amidst the general tension, the sorcerer placed one basket on the chest of the groom and the other on the breast of the bride. The Judgement of the Ants began.

"There are tiny holes in the baskets," Fujudi explained to me through Arnak. "The ants cannot escape, but they can bite through the openings. Look, they have begun already!"

It was obvious from the faces of the poor bride and groom that the ants had not been idle. Sweat was pouring off both copiously, and both were biting their lips, though they did it surreptitiously so as not to betray their pain.

"The point is," explained Fujudi, "that they must bear the pain bravely and with great calm. Let either one as much as move in pain, or worse yet, cry out, and it is over."

"What is over?"

"They cannot marry! And they will cover themselves with shame!"

"They cannot marry?" I returned to Arnak. "They will not be able to live together?"

"Oh, but they have lived together for some time, only secretly. Now, they will live openly, build a hut, and eat together by their own fire. She will cultivate his corn and cassava, and he will bring her fish and game."

"And they will have children."

"Oh, they have children already. But if they shout out now, it will be a great disgrace."

The sorcerer was not taking it easy on the young couple. Every now and then, he picked up one basket or the other, shook it to goad the ants, and always set it back on a different body part. The drum, meanwhile, was beating its dull accompaniment, gradually increasing its speed and volume, ever more furious, and the people watched the young victims with ever greater, merciless curiosity. Their eyes shone again, but I no longer knew why: from too much drink or from excess of cruelty.

The rite came to a crescendo when the sorcerer opened the baskets and poured their contents over the bodies of the newlyweds. There were so many ants that they covered the young couple's skin with a black, thick layer of crawling, biting beasts. The ants quickly spread everywhere, and there was no uncovered place on the tormented bodies that they did not bite and inject with venom.

The young people hung on bravely and did not budge. He got a bigger portion of the ants, and sometimes, he seemed to me to be losing consciousness. The biting insects crawled on their faces, too, and the afflicted had to close their eyelids lest the insects eat their eyes away. But even so, they endured the pain beyond anything I would have been prepared to take. Only the woman's eyes began to run with tears from under her tightly closed eyelids, but she neither sighed nor moved. After a while, the ants began to leave their bodies and scatter on the pier.

The sorcerer announced that the newlyweds had passed the test. But then, some unruly youths shouted indignantly: "She did not pass the test because she was all in tears! They cannot marry!" But others stood up in defense of the newlyweds. There was a stir and raised voices, and only because of our presence did it not end up in a proper fight. Soon, the calmer Warao prevailed over the brawlers and appeased the envious with generous helpings of *kashiri*. And now peace and harmony were reestablished. The young couple were free to marry.

"Did you see the mess?" asked Arnak in a hushed voice, even though no one here except Vagura understood English.

"What? The ant rite?"

"No, the argument! You know what it shows?"

"Yes?"

"That their sorcerer is a wimp and a loser if his people dare to stand up against his judgment."

"You think?"

"Oh, yes! Such insubordination would not have happened in any other tribe. What the sorcerer says is sacred! The sorcerer is more powerful than a chief. But this one?!"

And Arnak shook his head in disapproval.

After the Judgment of the Ants, the party resumed even louder than before, for now, it became a wedding celebration. For us, the elders, hammocks were hung up, and I was told to climb into one myself. I must admit that it was unexpectedly comfortable.

*Kashiri* went into circulation again, but I only pretended to drink. Not so, my comrades. Luckily, Arnak, Vagura, and Lasana drank almost nothing and watched over the others. Still, more than one of our men, drunk to the point of stupor, had to be carried to the ship to sleep there.

I very much liked the sober discipline of the Africans. Seeing that almost all the Arawaks were drunk and that it was mainly an Indian celebration, Miguel and the rest of the Africans withdrew to the schooner, and there they made sure that no unauthorized person could get at our property.

Meanwhile, Manauri, feeling in seventh heaven, did not abstain from drink. Drunk and lying next to me, he engaged in a lively chat with Jekuana with the help of Fujudi. The two chiefs had important secrets to share, for Jekuana now burst into gaiety less often, sometimes frowned, and from time to time, cast sidelong glances at me. Finally, he climbed down from his hammock and, pulling up a stool, sat down next to me.

"*Anau*, Great Chief, wise White Jaguar!" he began in a singsong voice, waving his arms over me, which evidently expressed his cordial feelings. "You're a wise leader. Mighty!"

"You're going to give me a big head," I laughed. "Manauri must have told you some fairy tale stories about me."

"Fairy tales?" repeated the Warao, slyly winking at me. "White Jaguar is modest! Don't you have many fire teeth that—*boom, boom!*—tear enemies to pieces?"

Here, Jekuana pointed with respect to my silver pistol, which I had put down in front of me."

"Yes, I have many such biting teeth!" I admitted, amused.

"And have you not persuaded your companions," continued the chief in the same flattering tone, "to learn how to bite with these fiery teeth?"

"This is also true," I admitted readily. "But look around you! My fiery teeth are terrible at biting, but your *kashiri*, though it is only a drink, has bitten my men!"

At these words, I looked eloquently at several drunk Arawaks. Everyone present roared with laughter, and Jekuana admitted with boastful regret that such was the nature of all Indians: they were all incorrigible drunks.

Wishing to direct our conversation in a more practical direction, I asked Jekuana what he knew about the English who supposedly lived at the mouth of the Essequibo River, where I wanted to go. But the chief deflected my question and went only so far as to admit that, indeed, somewhere in the south, there were English people and that they were much kinder to the Indians than the Dutch, but the Dutch were more numerous and far worse,

"Oh, the Dutch!" shuddered Jekuana at a thought that crossed his mind.

"Do they bother you?"

"And how! They themselves—no, but their thugs, the slave catchers!"

And here he suddenly stopped, as if he had said too much.

"You, White Jaguar," he turned to me in a pleading voice. "You go west now, to the Imataca River, not south to the English. With us, the Warao, and with the Arawaks on the Imataca, you will find love, and friendship, and favor because you arrive in a special moment, and we are especially happy to welcome you now. Now, you will find sincere friends here."

"And what is so special about this moment?"

Jekuana again dodged the question, pretending he hadn't heard it—or perhaps he was too tipsy. Once in a while, he clapped his hands, summoned to him serving women, ordered more food, fruit, and *kashiri*.

The women who served us were mostly flighty teenage girls. Like eager prancing deer, they jumped around us, but among them, there were also more mature girls, just as frivolous as the young. Two knelt by my hammock and chirped at me confusedly, like two lovely birds.

"What do they want?" I asked my companions.

Fujudi laughed.

"They are flirting with you!"

"Flirting? What are they saying?"

"They say that for you, they would not be afraid of a couple of ants."

We all laughed at the joke, but after a moment, Lasana, smiling but firm, grabbed the two young suitors by the neck and drove them away.

The descending sun was already touching the tops of the trees. The day was quickly fading. Jekuana was very curious to see all our weapons, so I took him to our ship and had the matchlocks carried aboard.

They impressed him. The chief admired our weapons with mute respect for a long while and finally asked when we would resume our journey.

"Tomorrow," I said. "At high tide."

"I will come with you."

"You will come with us?"

"Yes! I will take you to Oronapi. I have already sent him word that you are coming."

"Oronapi... Who is Oronapi?"

"He is the chief of all the Warao in these parts."

"But my comrades and I are in a hurry to reach the Imataca," I reminded him.

"That is perfect! The headquarters of Oronapi, Kaiiwa, lies on your way, on the banks of the Orinoco, two days' journey from here."

"Then we can stop there."

Jekuana clearly attached extraordinary importance to that visit.

Later, he took me by the arm and led me a short distance to the bank of the river, where several boats lay half-drawn out of the water. Some were small, made of tree bark, while others were much larger, made of whole tree trunks with burnt-out hollows. The chief said he would give me one of the big ones and that I should choose the one I liked. Such a boat, which could accommodate twenty or more men, represented real capital, so Jekuana's unexpected generosity surprised my Arawaks, and they did not want to accept the gift.

"Nothing extraordinary about it!" the chief explained. "Your three Spanish boats are too heavy for these waters. You need a long, narrow boat to deal with the tides and the current, a boat as quick as an arrow. And, anyway," he added with a mysterious smile, "in war, only Indian boats are useful."

"War? Are you trying to frighten me?"

"I would never try to frighten you, White Jaguar. But in this forest, war lurks behind every bush, and no one can escape it, not even you. Therefore, you better have a swift boat."

And he exploded again in such extraordinary gaiety that I was not sure how to interpret his strange words. Not wanting to remain in his debt, I invited him to choose for himself a weapon from our inventory. He chose a Spanish sword, the emblem of a commander's authority, much more eloquent and explicit than a matchlock.

As I lay on the deck, falling asleep, and went over the events of the day, I marveled at the hospitality of the Warao. There was something bewildering about their unexpected feelings for me. Just like the scent of the mud and rotting plants coming from the nearby forest and the shrill cries of the nocturnal beasts, it dazed my senses. It deafened them.

**END OF EPISODE 2**

## TRANSLATOR'S SPECIAL REQUEST

Translating and publishing this book has been a labor of love for me.
I grew up reading it, and I have always wanted to be able
to share it with my American friends. And so here it is.
It will not make me rich, but if you liked the book, would you please
recommend it to a friend?
And give it an Amazon review?
https://www.amazon.com/dp/2919820494

THANK YOU!

Witold Makowiecki

# Wind from the Hospitable Sea

Greece 562 BC. For insolvent debtors, the price of bankruptcy is slavery. When his mother and siblings are seized for unpaid debts, little Diossos must run to fetch help. He must cross mountains, forests, and stormy seas, brave wild animals, slave catchers, pirates, and... the law. He has one month to achieve his quest but only days to grow up.

Maria Rodziewiczówna

# A Summer of the Forest Folk

The most beautiful book you will read this year.
Turn of the nineteenth century. Three women spend their summers in a remote cottage deep in the last virgin forest in Europe. This summer, their teenage big-city nephew joins them. A heart-warming, feel-good tale of love and friendship, of coming of age, and of the healing power of nature. This is a book like nothing you have ever read, a phenomenon, a genre of its own.

## Aleksander Krawczuk

An international cult figure among East European lovers of antiquity. A scholar, professor at the Jagiellonian University, minister of culture of Poland (1986-1989), and author of 30 popular books on the antique.

His delightful books, written in a conversational, highly readable style, often in an unusual literary format, appeal to the general public as much as they do to serious students of history. "A.K." became a phenomenon, a cultural icon: at one point, he hosted his own internationally syndicated TV program. And yet, for political reasons, his delightful works appear in English only now.

# Seven Against Thebes

Before the Trojan War, there was the Theban War. Who fought it? Why? What does archeology tell us, and what has survived of ancient the epics?

# The Last Olympiad

Serapeum destroyed! Emperor murdered! Pagans raise a revolt! Read leading lights of their time (389-395 AD) as they debate everything from bathing to demon possession.

# A Meeting in Oea

Meet Apuleius, Rome's all-time best-selling author, a Platonic scholar, a part-time magician, and a dowry-hunter, as he works on his treatise on Plato at night and schemes to marry a rich African widow by day.

# Titus and Berenice

The last vestiges of the kingdom of Judah hung for a while on the outcome of the love affair between the elderly Jewish queen Berenice, granddaughter of Herod the Great, and the 12 years younger son of Vespasian, the emperor of Rome.

Jacek Bocheński
*The Notorious Roman Trilogy*

# Divine Julius

"Would you like to become a god? It has been done before. There are techniques." A great literary success at the time of its first appearance, the book was almost immediately banned by the Communist regime. More recently, it was banned by Facebook because "it might affect the way our users vote."

*The Polish classic. Pure magnificence. This should not be read; it should be savored. It is a filet mignon.*

ISBN: 978-9998793781

# Naso the Poet

The loves and crimes of Rome's greatest poet. This beautifully and wittily told story of Ovid was subjected to thousands of censorship edits, thereby becoming possibly the world's most heavily censored book.

*It would be difficult to find a more brilliant fictional treatment of Ovid's life than this hilariously serious entertainment.*

ISBN: 978-2919820047

# Tiberius Caesar

The horrifying tale of Tiberius Caesar, the second emperor of Rome: the man who normalized political terror. A moral, intellectual, emotional zero whose only skill in life was to grab and hang onto power. Be very afraid.

ISBN: 978-2919820047